NorthParadePublishing

©2018 North Parade Publishing Ltd.
4 North Parade,
Bath BA11LF. UK
Printed in China.
www.nppbooks.co.uk

Picture credits

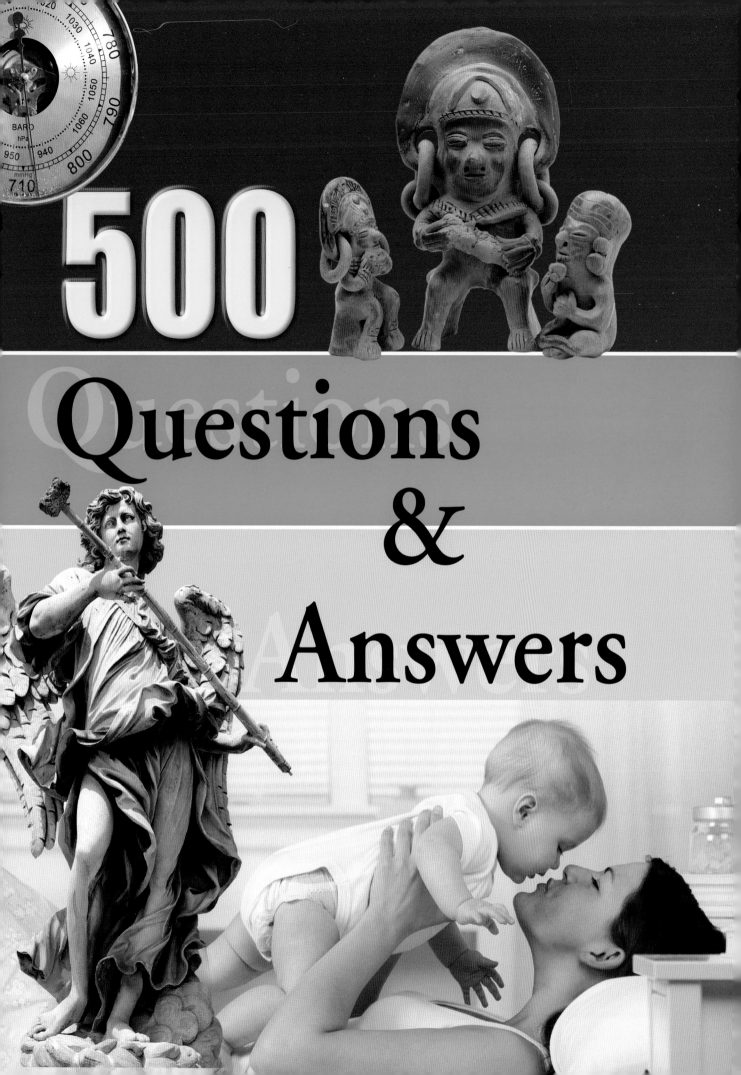

500
Questions
&
Answers

INTRODUCTION TO UNIVERSE AND GALAXIES

Do you know how old and big our Universe is?

Our universe, a vast, undefined expanse of space that contains all the matter and energy that exists, is 13.7 billion years old or so the scientists say! And if the age surprises you, wait till you read about its size – our Universe is said to be 13.7 billion light years in radius. Do you know how the astronomers estimated the size? They got it by multiplying the age of the universe by the speed of light!

And what is a light year? Why do scientists measure distances in the universe in light years?

A light year is the distance travelled by light in a year. That's simple but how much do you think that distance would be? It is around 9,500,000,000,000km! Eleven zeros! That is quite a distance light travels, but doesn't get tired by the end of the journey! Imagine having to use kilometres to measure the universe – wouldn't that be difficult? Scientists use light years when measuring distances in the universe because it is more practical to use this measurement unit. Parsec is another measurement unit commonly used. A Parsec is equal to 3.3 light years.

But how did the Universe come into being?

There are many theories that have been proposed to explain the formation of the universe. The most popular theory is the 'Big Bang' theory. About 13 billion years ago, the Universe got so hot that it started expanding, similar to a balloon, at a tremendous speed. The expansion caused it to cool down and created our ever-expanding Universe. Yes, our Universe is still expanding!

What all is our Universe made of?

Our Universe is made up of innumerable galaxies and its components such as the stars, planets, dust and gas.

Galaxy refers to a cluster of stars, gas and dust held together. And what holds them together – gravitational force, which acts like glue. Galaxies vary in size and are scattered throughout the universe. Galaxies can occur singly or in groups that are called 'super clusters'.

Do you know which category our galaxy belongs to? Our Milky Way is a Spiral Galaxy!

That begs a question, what is a spiral galaxy?

There are three kinds of galaxies – Irregular galaxies which have undefined shapes and consist of young stars, dust and gas; spiral galaxies, which are shaped like discs, most of which resemble a pin-wheel, with the arms of the galaxies spiraling outward as it rotates. These type of galaxies contain middle-aged stars and clouds of gas and dust; and elliptical galaxies which vary from round to elongated spheres and contain old stars and very little gas or dust.

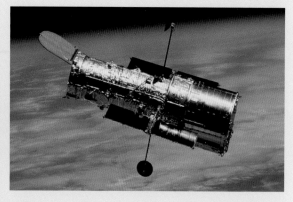

What is the Hubble telescope?

The Hubble Space Telescope is a large and optically superior telescope that was put into orbit by the space shuttle, Discovery, in April 1990. Since it is orbiting above the Earth's murky atmosphere, the pictures are much clearer than the ones taken from Earth. The Hubble telescope was named after Edward Hubble who first discovered the expansion of universe. Thanks to the pictures taken by the Hubble telescope, scientists are now able to learn exciting new things - the size and age of the universe, how galaxies form, and about explosions when stars die!

Is there a black hole in Milky Way?

Scientists have discovered a black hole in the centre of Milky Way, but there is no need to panic! It is located about 24,000 light years away from the Earth and at that distance it does not really pose any danger to us!

Are any galaxies visible to the naked eye?

On Earth, three galaxies are visible to the unaided eye! The Andromeda Nebula can be seen in the skies in the Northern Hemisphere. The Large and the Small Magellanic Clouds are visible from the Southern Hemisphere. Look out for them, next time you gaze at the sky!

How large is the Milky Way galaxy and where is our Solar System located in it?

Our pinwheel-shaped galaxy, the Milky Way, is a spiral galaxy approximately 100,000 light years in diameter. The Milky Way is believed to have formed about 14 billion years ago. Our Solar system is located about 26,000 light years from the

STARS

What is a star made of?

The bright stars we see in the sky are made of gases like hydrogen and helium and also stellar dust! A star produces and emits light because of the nuclear fusion reaction of hydrogen and helium in its core. The energy generated in the core provides the pressure necessary to prevent the star from collapsing due to its own weight. Do you know the star closest to our Earth? It is the Sun!

How is a star formed?

A star is formed from a nebula, which is a cloud of gas and dust. The cloud collapses under its own gravitational attraction and the core starts heating up and gives rise to a 'proto star'. It is this proto star which eventually becomes a star after gathering more gas and dust. How long does a star take to grow up? Quite long! A star about the size of our Sun will need about 50 million years to mature from the beginning stages to adulthood!

Why do stars twinkle and why do some stars in the sky appear bright while others appear dim?

Ever gazed at the sky admiring the beautiful twinkling stars? Stars do not actually twinkle but just appear to, when observed from the Earth's surface due to the effect of the atmosphere. When light from a star enters the atmosphere, it is affected by the factors like wind and temperature that causes the twinkling effect. Stars come in varying sizes and brightness levels. A star appears bright or dim depending on its distance from Earth. The brightness of a star also depends on its size too. A larger star will appear brighter than a smaller one.

Do stars change colour?

The colour of stars depends on their temperature which in turn depends on the changes happening on the surface of the star. As a star evolves and pass through different phases, it experiences changes in temperature and hence a change in colour. For example, towards the end of a star's life, the temperature of the core increases, and it starts converting helium into hydrogen. The star then expands to become a red giant.

What is a constellation?

A constellation is a group of stars that appear close together and form a particular imaginary pattern.

If you have looked up at the sky, you might also have seen stars forming strange shapes! However these stars may be light years away and not related to each other in any way. There are 88 officially recognized constellations. Different constellations are visible from different hemispheres of the Earth and at different times of the year.

Which is the star nearest to our Solar System?

Proxima Centauri is the nearest star to our Solar System. This star is a part of a triple star system which includes Alpha Centauri A and Alpha Centauri B. Our neighbor, Proxima Centauri, is about one tenth the size of the Sun and is located about 4.3 light years away!

What is a nova and supernova?

A nova refers to the phenomenon of sudden brightening of a star. It occurs when a white dwarf star is in close proximity to another star. In such a case, the white dwarf can pull material from the other star and nuclear fusion might occur causing a rise in temperature and subsequently brightness. Ancient astronomers who did not have modern equipment and technology of today, simply observed a new star in a place where there were no stars before. This was how it got the name - 'Stella Nova' which means 'New Star'. Supernova refers to the brightness observed when a massive star dies and explodes. Do you know that sometimes the light emitted by a supernova is so bright that it can outshine the whole galaxy!

What are neutron stars and pulsars?

Neutron stars are remnants of particular types of supernovae. They typically have diameter of about 20 km and mass greater than three times that of Sun. Neutron stars rotate rapidly and have very intense magnetic fields. They are the densest objects known to us! Pulsars are rapidly rotating neutron stars whose emitted electromagnetic radiation is observed as pulses.

What is a black hole?

A black hole is an area in space with gravity so strong that even light cannot escape from it! A black hole forms in the centre of galaxies or when a giant star collapses and shrinks. The material from the star is trapped in an infinitely small space, thus greatly increasing the gravity. When matter gets packed so densely that even light cannot escape, it is referred to as a black hole.

What is beyond the planets? The Kuiper Belt, which is a disc-shaped region of icy objects, extends beyond the orbit of Neptune. The Oort cloud, which is farther away from the Kuiper Belt, is believed to consist of comets that orbit the sun.

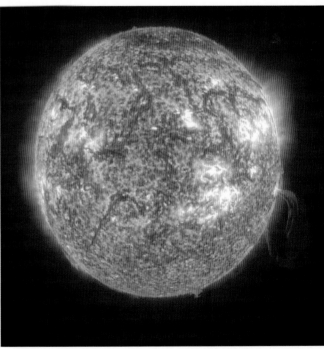

What is the Solar System?

The Solar System is the Sun's own family! It comprises of the Sun, the planets and other celestial bodies that orbit around it. The components of the Solar System include the planets, their satellites, comets and asteroids which are held together by the gravitational force from the Sun.

How big is the Solar System?

The size of the Solar System is estimated to be 40 AU (Astronomical Units) up to the orbit of Pluto. (One AU is roughly the distance between the Earth and Sun which is 150,000,000,000 metres.)

What type of a star is the sun?

The sun is a yellow dwarf star considered to be about 4 billion years old. The core of the sun is hot because nuclear fusion reactions occur, generating great amounts of energy. This energy radiates into space as light and heat, and thanks to the Sun, it is possible for us to live on Earth!

How hot is the Sun?

The temperature on the outer surface of the Sun, called the Photosphere, is around 5000 °C (11,000 °F). If you think that is hot, then the temperature at the core of the Sun is as high as 15,000,000 °C (27,000,000 °F)!

Does the Sun rotate around its axis?

Just like the planets, the Sun does rotate around its axis. It rotates faster at its equator than at the poles. Scientists discovered this by observing the change in sunspots and other features on the surface of the Sun!

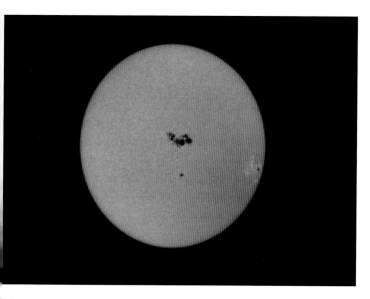

What are sunspots?

Sunspots are magnetic storms on the surface of the Sun which appear as darker areas on the Sun. On an average, a sunspot can be hundreds of thousands of miles long, many times larger than the earth. The temperature of a sunspot is approximately 1500 °C cooler than the surrounding area.

What is the size of the sun in comparison to our planet Earth?

The Sun has a diameter of 864,400 miles, which is about 109 times that of Earth. To get an idea, it is so large that about 1,300,000 Earths can fit snugly inside it!

What is a solar eclipse?

A solar eclipse is a phenomenon that occurs when the moon moves in between the sun and the earth. The moon covers the sun entirely during a total solar eclipse as seen from earth. A partial eclipse will occur when the sun, earth and moon are not lined up precisely.

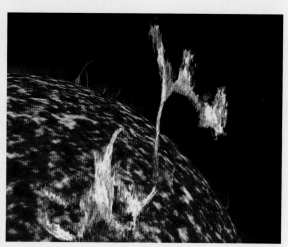

What is a solar flare?

A solar flare is a sudden and rapid increase in brightness in a region on the surface of the sun. It occurs when the magnetic energy built up on the surface of the sun is suddenly released. The energy released during a typical solar flare is so powerful – It is equivalent to millions of 100 megaton hydrogen bombs exploding at the same time! Mind-blowing, isn't it?

PLANETS

How were the planets formed?

Our star and the planets were formed from a collapsing cloud of gas and dust within a larger cloud called nebula. As more material was pulled within the cloud due to gravity, the centre became hot and dense forming the kernel of a star. The remaining gas and dust got flattened into a proto-planetary disc, that collected more mass and became planets.

What are rocky planets?

The inner planets – Mercury, Venus, Earth and Mars – are referred to as the 'terrestrial' or 'rocky' planets. These planets are composed of rock and heavy metals. The terrestrial planets are much smaller than the gas planets and have few or no moons.

What about the rest of the planets?

The outer planets Jupiter, Saturn, Uranus and Neptune are collectively referred to as the 'gas giants'. These planets are composed mainly of gas and have a rocky core made of molten heavy metals. Gas giants are massive but despite their size, they have low densities. These planets have many moons and planetary rings.

What are dwarf planets?

Dwarf planets are a relatively new classification of astronomical objects. Pluto, Ceres, Eris, Haumea and Makemake constitute the dwarf planets. Pluto, Eris, Haumea and Makemake are found in the outer solar system in the Kuiper belt. The dwarf planet, Ceres, is found in the asteroid belt between Mars and Jupiter! Quite a rocky neighbourhood!

Planet	Surface/Atmosphere composition	Colour
Mercury	Silicate rocks and dust	Dark Grey
Venus	Carbon dioxide and sulphuric acid clouds	Light yellow
Earth	Oceans, Clouds, Land, vegetation	Blue, white, brown and green
Mars	Iron oxide dust (rust)	Orange
Jupiter	Hydrogen, helium, water droplets, ammonia	Whit, orange, brown and red
Saturn	Hydrogen, helium, water vapour, ammonia, phosphine, hydrocarbons	Yellowish brown
Uranus	Methane, hydrogen, helium	greenish blue
Neptune	Hydrogen, helium, methane	Blue

Which is the largest planet in our Solar System?

Jupiter is the largest planet in our Solar System. It has a diameter of 142,000 km which is about 11 times that of Earth. About 1300 Earths could fit inside Jupiter! Put together all the other planets in the Solar System and Jupiter would still weigh two and half times more than all the planets!

Do all planets have moons like Earth?

Some planets have no moons while others have many moons! Moons are natural satellites that revolve around planets in specific orbits. They are smaller than the planet and vary in size and shape.

Planet	Number of Moons	Planet	Number of Moons
Mercury	0	Jupiter	63
Venus	0	Saturn	60
Earth	1	Uranus	27
Mars	2	Neptune	13

What is the Great Red Spot on Jupiter?

The Great Red Spot seen on the surface of Jupiter is actually a giant spinning storm that has been observed through telescopes, even 400 years ago! Winds inside the storm reach speeds close to 270 miles per hour, much faster and stronger than any winds on Earth! The Great Red Spot is more than 2 times the size of Earth!

How does the rotation of Venus differ from the other planets?

Venus is the only planet in the Solar system that rotates in clockwise direction. Venus is also slowest spinning planet in the Solar System. In fact, Venus holds a very unique record – on this planet a day is longer than a year! It takes Venus 243 Earth days to spin once around its axis while it takes only 225 days to revolve once around the Sun.

What are the rings around planet Saturn composed of?

The stunning rings around the planet Saturn are made of pieces of ice, rocks and dust. The size of these pieces vary greatly and they are held together by gravity. The rings are about 270,000 km in diameter but only a few hundred metres thick!

How large is the Earth and how much does it weigh?

Earth has a diameter of 12,756 km when measured at the equator and 12,725 km when measured around the poles. This is because Earth is an elongated sphere, bulging slightly at the center than at the poles. There is no weighing scales that can measure the Earth, so using mathematical calculations and the laws of gravity, scientists have determined the weight to be about 13,170,000,000,000,000,000,000,000 lbs!

What makes Earth unique among other planets in the Solar System?

There are many reasons why Earth is very unique and special in the Solar System:

- It is the only planet that has liquid water on its surface

- Earth has sustained life forms (as we know it) for about 3.9 billion years

- Earth is protected from harmful radiation by the protective layer

- Earth is stabilized by the presence of a large moon

Where is Earth located in the Universe?

Want to know the full address of Planet Earth? Earth is the third planet from the Sun in the Solar System. The Solar system is located in the spiral arm of the Milky Way galaxy called Orion Arm. The Milky Way is located in a small group of galaxies called the 'Local Group' in the Virgo Supercluster of galaxies. (A Supercluster refers to a group of galaxies held together by gravity.)

How old is the Earth?

Scientists have predicted the age of the Earth to be somewhere between 4.5 and 4.8 billion years. The age of the Earth is measured by calculating the rate at which radioactive uranium breaks down into lead in very old rocks on Earth.

How does the Moon help stabilize the Earth?

The Moon is the only natural satellite of Earth and it rotates around the Earth in a slightly elliptical orbit. It is believed that the Moon was formed from the debris that resulted from the collision of an astronomical object, the size of Mars, with Earth, very long ago! The Moon is responsible for stabilizing the planet from wobbling on its axis thus leading to uniform climates.

How far is the moon from Earth?

The moon is situated at an average distance of 384,000 km away from the Earth. Did you know that the first spacecraft to the Moon, Luna 1, took about 3 days to reach the Moon from Earth!

What is the size of the moon in comparison to earth?

The moon has a diameter of 3476 km and is about one fourth the size of Earth. The moon weighs 80 times less than the Earth.

What is a lunar eclipse?

A lunar eclipse occurs when the Earth passes between the sun and the moon, thus blocking sunlight from striking the surface of the moon. Since the moon does not emit light on its own, it appears dark during an eclipse.

What do studies of rocks brought from Moon reveal?

Astronauts brought back pounds of moon rocks from their moon trips! Analysis and studies of rocks brought from the moon have helped scientists predict how the moon could have formed. It has also provided information about the surface composition of moon and helped conclude that there is no liquid water on the surface.

COMETS, METEORITES AND ASTEROIDS

What are comets?

Comets are astronomical objects that are made of ice crystals of water, carbon dioxide, ammonia, methane and dust. They are commonly referred to as 'dirty snowballs'!

Why do comets have tails?

Do you know how a comet's tail is formed? When a comet come close to sun, the ice in the nucleus of the comet gets heated up and vaporizes to form a trail of gas and dust that looks like a tail and this tail is referred to as a 'coma'. The tail of a comet is formed in a direction away from the Sun and stretches for millions of kilometres!

What is Halley's Comet?

Halley's Comet, named after the English astronomer, Edmund Halley, who studied it, was the first comet whose return was predicted. Want to see the Halley's Comet? You'll have to wait until 2062!

What is a meteor shower?

A meteor shower is observed when the Earth passes through the orbit of a comet. When this occurs, small comet debris, no larger than grains of sand enter the Earth's atmosphere and get burned up. This results in streaks of light that can be observed in the night sky.

What are meteorites?

Meteorites are considered to be remnants of comets or asteroids that survive the fall through Earth's atmosphere. There are three major types of meteorites: stone meteorites that are made of silicate material, iron meteorites which have a major composition of iron and a significant amount of nickel, and stony-iron meteorites that are a mixture of stone and iron material.

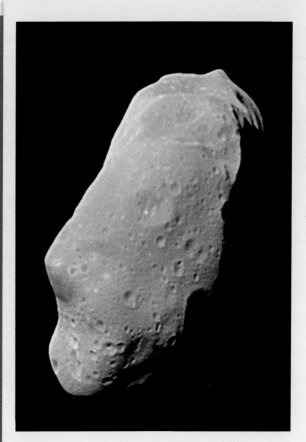

How is an asteroid different from a comet?

Asteroids differ from comets in their composition. While asteroids are primarily made of metals and rocky material, comets are made of ice, rocky material and dust. Scientists believe that asteroids formed much closer to Sun and comets farther away from the sun.

Where is the asteroid belt located in our Solar System?

The asteroid belt is located between Mars and Jupiter and contains millions of meteoroids of different sizes. Most of the asteroids found in the Solar system are in this belt region. Sometimes large asteroids can collide with one another and result in the formation of smaller asteroids. Asteroids are sometimes pulled out of their orbit by the gravitational attraction of planets.

What is the difference between a meteoroid and a meteorite?

As long as they are moving through space, these astronomical objects are called meteoroids. Meteoroids that fall on Earth or other celestial bodies are called meteorites.

What is an asteroid?

Asteroids are rocky metallic astronomical objects that can vary in size from centimetres to kilometres! Asteroids are thought to be remnants from formation of the Solar System. Who said only planets can have moons? Like planets, asteroids also can have moons!

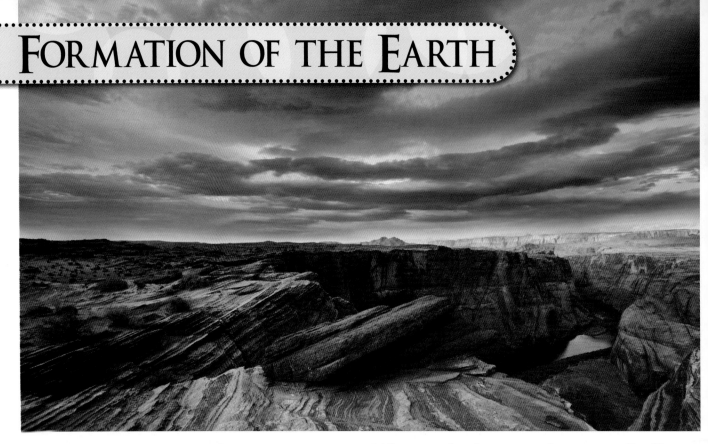

How did our Earth form?

The Sun and the planets, including the Earth, were formed from a rapidly spinning disc of dust and gas. The centre of the disc became the sun and the planets developed from spheres of dust, gas and molten liquid that eventually cooled and became solid. It is believed that an object the size of Mars collided with Earth, leaving behind a huge gap that might have left room for oceans.

What about the Earth's atmosphere?

Scientists believe that the Earth's atmosphere evolved over millions of years! The first atmosphere consisted only of hydrogen and helium which eventually escaped Earth's gravity. The second atmosphere was formed as a result of intense volcanic activities on Earth that released steam, ammonia and carbon dioxide. After much of the carbon dioxide dissolved in oceans, a simple life form evolved that could utilize this dissolved carbon dioxide and sunlight. These life forms released oxygen which began accumulating in the atmosphere. The sunlight broke down ammonia into nitrogen and hydrogen. Hydrogen, being light, drifted away leaving behind the atmosphere we have today- carbon dioxide, oxygen and nitrogen.

What is the layer we live on called?

The outermost layer of the Earth is called the 'crust' and it comprises the continents where we live and the ocean basins. After formation, the earth began to cool and during this process iron and nickel accumulated in the core while silicates rich in aluminium began to accumulate on the surface forming a thin layer known as the crust. The crust which holds us constitutes less than one percent of the Earth's composition!

Did the continents always look the way they do today?

The continents we see today were very different long ago! About 250 million years ago, the large supercontinent 'Pangaea' underwent continental drift and fragmentation to form 'Laurasia' in the north and 'Gondwanaland' in the south. Laurasia included present day North America, Europe and Asia except India. Gondwanaland included present day Africa, South America, India, Australia and Antarctica. These two supercontinents were separated by a strip of Ocean called 'Tethys'. Continuous movement and change has resulted in the continents we see today.

When did life begin on Earth?

Though the exact process by which the first life forms originated is not known, scientists believe that life originated on Earth about 3 billion years

ago – only when the bombardment of Earth by comets and asteroids finally ended! Subsequent less intense collisions of comets, are believed to have provided carbon-based molecules and water needed for the creation of life forms!

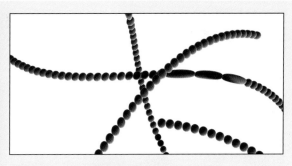

What are the first life-forms that lived on Earth?

The first life-forms are considered to be primitive, single-celled organisms called cyanobacteria. It is believed that these organisms made use of sunlight and carbon dioxide in the Earth's atmosphere, in a process called photosynthesis, to survive and reproduce and released oxygen as a waste product. After 2 billion years, these single-celled organisms evolved into more complex, multi-cellular organisms. There are other theories that suggest that the first life forms might have been 'heterotrophs' – organisms that used organic molecules available from the surroundings for energy. It is thanks to these organisms that we are alive today!

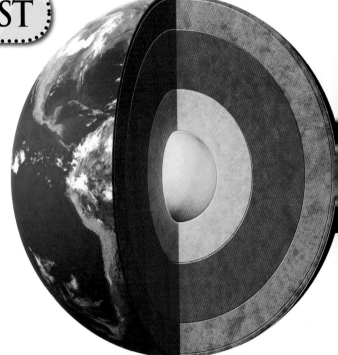

What is geology?

Geology is the study of the Earth, its composition, the natural land formations and the processes that act upon them. An extended arm of geology called 'historical geology' deals with studying materials that form the Earth, natural structures, processes, climate and how organisms have changed over time. This includes learning when dinosaurs lived and how they were wiped out and lots of other interesting things!

Does the Earth have different layers?

A cross-section of the earth would reveal the following layers:

- Core: The core is the most interior part of the Earth and is divided into two sections – the outer core and the inner core. The outer core is liquid and consists of iron, nickel and sulphur. The inner core is solid and consists mainly of iron.

- Mantle: The middle layer is the mantle which is about 2900 km in thickness and divided into two sections – the upper mantle and the lower mantle. It is composed of ferro-magnesium silicates. Most of the internal heat of the Earth is located in this region.

- Crust: The outermost, thin layer of Earth which holds the ocean basins and the continents is the crust. The crust is made of aluminum silicates and varies in thickness from 5-10 km in ocean basins to 35-70 km in continents.

Why is the Earth's surface constantly in motion?

Did you know that the surface of the Earth is continuously moving? The Earth's lithosphere, which consists of the crust and the upper mantle, is divided into a number of segments called 'plates'. These plates move in relation to one another and this phenomenon is known as 'plate tectonics'. Geologists believe that in the upper mantle might be responsible for circulating heat and causing these movements.

What are seismic waves?

It is common to hear people talking about seismic waves in relation to earthquakes. What exactly are these seismic waves? Seismic waves are energy waves caused during the sudden breaking or explosion of rock within the Earth's surface. These shock waves travel through the Earth's surface and can be detected through recordings on seismographs. The two major types of seismic waves are body waves and surface waves. Body waves can travel through the inner layers of Earth while surface waves move along the surface of the planet, similar to ripples along the water surface.

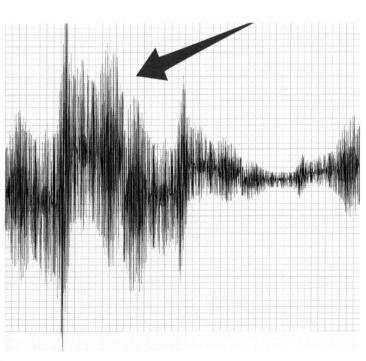

Do rocks remain the same throughout their existence of Earth?

No! The rocks of the earth continually change and are recycled over millions of years by processes such as erosion, volcanic eruption, immense heat and pressure. For example, sedimentary rocks may be transformed into metamorphic rocks. These may in turn be eroded and carried away by a river to form newer sedimentary rocks. This is known as the rock cycle.

What are the different types of rocks found on Earth?

The three major kinds of rocks found on Earth are Igneous, Metamorphic and Sedimentary rocks. Igneous rocks are formed by the cooling and solidifying of magma. Basalt and granite are examples. Rocks that have changed into other rocks due to massive heat and/or pressure are called metamorphic rocks. Examples include marble and slate. Compressed sediments form sedimentary rocks. Chalk and clay are sedimentary rocks.

How does the atmosphere protect the Earth?

The atmosphere is a protective layer of gases that acts as a shield for the earth by filtering harmful ultraviolet radiation from the sun and from meteorites, which usually get burned up while passing through the atmospheric layers! The atmosphere also provides oxygen and carbon dioxide needed for survival and reproduction of living things.

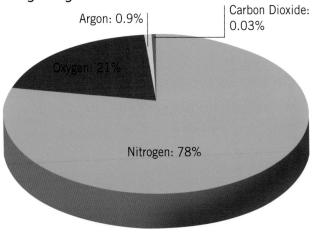

What is the atmosphere made of?

The atmosphere consists of the following gases: Nitrogen – 78 percent, Oxygen – 21 percent, Argon – 0.9 percent, Carbon Dioxide – 0.03 percent and traces of water vapour and rare gases like neon, krypton, xenon and helium.

Does the atmosphere have layers?

The atmosphere consists of four major layers – the troposphere, the stratosphere, the mesosphere and the thermosphere. The troposphere is the layer closest to Earth's surface and contains 75 percent of the gases. The lower region of the stratosphere consists of the protective ozone layer. The mesosphere is the coldest region of the atmosphere and helps protect Earth from falling meteorites. The thermosphere is the outermost layer which includes the ionosphere and the exosphere. The ionosphere contains charged particles and the satellites are found in the exosphere region where the air is very thin.

How is the ozone layer useful to us?

The ozone layer is found in the lower stratosphere region of the atmosphere and contains high concentrations of ozone, a molecule with three oxygen atoms. This layer protects the Earth from harmful ultraviolet radiation from the sun.

What will happen if the ozone layer thins out?

Depletion or thinning of the ozone layer can cause serious health risks to humans and other living organisms. It can increase incidences of skin cancer and cataracts. It will also reduce the plankton population in the oceans and affect biodiversity and agriculture.

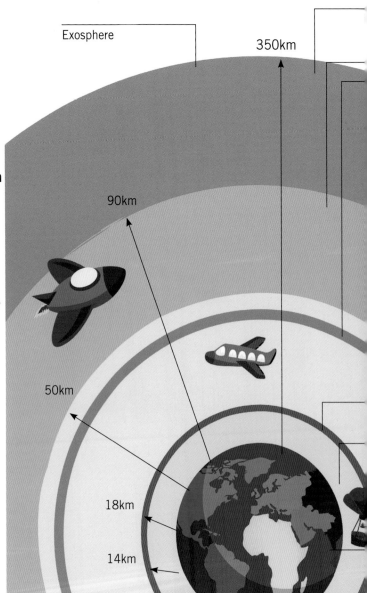

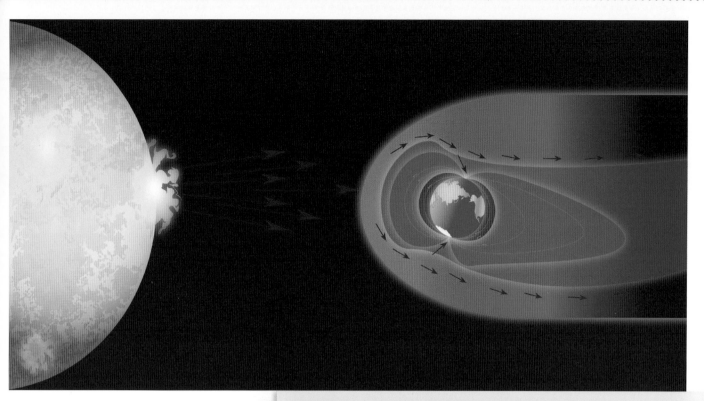

onosphere (Aurora)

Mesosphere

Ozone layer

Stratosphere

Tropopause

Troposphere

Earth

What is found beyond the atmosphere?

The region that extends beyond the atmosphere is called the magnetosphere. It begins at about 1000 km above the earth's surface and consists of electrons and protons. The harmful ultraviolet radiation from the Sun gets trapped in belts called the 'Van Allen Belts' in this layer.

The particles from a solar flare collide with each other in this region and result in a remarkable display of lights called, in the northern hemisphere, the 'Northern lights' or 'Aurora Borealis'.

25

WATER, RIVERS AND OCEANS

Is there a name for all the water stored on Earth?

Hydrosphere is the region where the water on Earth is stored in different forms like oceans, lakes, rivers, groundwater, snowfields, glaciers and the atmosphere. The water moves across the hydrosphere through various processes like evaporation, condensation, precipitation, transpiration, sublimation, infiltration, runoff, deposition and groundwater flow.

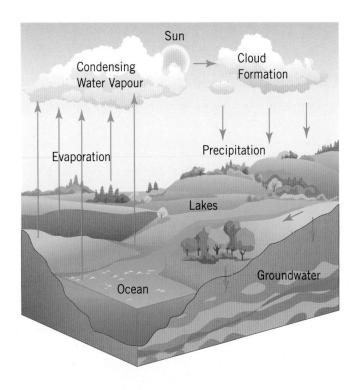

Why is there so much salt in the seas and oceans?

Oceans and seas contain about 35 parts of salt for every 1000 parts of water. The ocean and sea water are salty because of the dissolved salts that were derived from underwater volcanic eruptions, gradual erosion and weathering of rocks and mineral washings from rain, rivers and streams.

How did the oceans form?

Scientists believe that colliding astronomical objects left behind basins where water could collect. The steam and water from volcanic eruptions and comets collected in the atmosphere and when the Earth cooled down, resulted in condensation and rainfall that continued for millions of years to form oceans. Scientists believe that constant bombardment of meteorites on earth's surface might have made it difficult for water to be retained in oceans and hence oceans must have vaporized and reformed many times.

What is the percent of freshwater on Earth?

Approximately 97 percent of the water on the Earth's surface is found in oceans and only 3 percent constitutes freshwater in the form of ice caps, glaciers, groundwater, lakes, moisture in soil, atmospheric water vapour, streams and rivers.

Which are the longest and largest rivers on Earth?

The River Nile that flows through the mountains of central Africa to the Mediterranean Sea is the longest river on Earth with a total length calculated to be 4,160 miles (6,695 km). The river floods regularly and deposits fertile sediments ideal for agriculture. The River Amazon that flows through South America is considered to be the largest river and the second longest river on earth. The river discharges about 4,200,000 cubic feet of water per second into the Atlantic Ocean!

What is an aquifer?

An aquifer is a natural formation of rock, gravel, silt or other material that stores water under the ground. Water wells can be dug to extract the groundwater from aquifers for use.

What is the place where a river meets the ocean called?

Delta is the soil-rich land formed at the place where a river enters the ocean. Large amounts of silt and sediments are deposited in the delta. The main channel of the river is divided into smaller sections that are referred to as distributaries.

How are clouds formed?

Clouds form when the water vapour present in a parcel of air condenses to liquid form. A cloud is composed of millions of water droplets or ice crystals in colder regions. It is very rare to find clouds in deserts because there is very little water vapour that can evaporate to form clouds.

BIOMES

What is a biome?

A biome is a large geographic area with characteristic vegetation and animal groups adapted to live in that region. The climate and geography of a particular terrain determines what type of biome can exist there. The survival of a biome depends on the ecological relationship and balance between the organisms in the biome.

What are the types of biomes?

The major types of biomes on land are: Tundra, Taiga, Forests (Temperate & Tropical), Grasslands, Mountains and Deserts.

What is the total area on Earth occupied by forests?

According to the most recent global assessment conducted by FAO in 2006, forests cover 30 percent of the land area on Earth. In 2005, the total forest area was estimated to be 4 billion hectares. Sadly, forests are continuously being cut down throughout the world!

Do forests have layers?

Forests have three distinct layers. The forest floor has all the decomposing plant and animal material. You can find ferns, grass and fungi growing here. Then comes the understory which includes all the bushes, shrubs and young trees. The top layer of the forest that includes tall trees and their branches forms the canopy layer. This layer gets the most sunlight.

What are the different types of mountains?

Curious about how different types of mountains are formed? Here are the major types of mountains:

- Fold Mountains: When two continental tectonic plates collide, the edges crumble and form fold mountains. The Alps, the Himalayas, and the Rocky Mountains are examples of Fold Mountains.

- Fault-block Mountains: These types of mountains are formed when faults or cracks on the Earth's surface force material to be pushed upwards. The Sierra Nevada Mountain is a good example.

- Dome Mountains: Formed when magma pushes up the Earth's crust from underneath. The Black Hills in South Dakota is an example.

- Volcanic Mountains: As the name suggests, are formed from magma that flows out from volcanic vents and builds up as layers. The Mauna Kea in Hawaii was formed in such a way.

- Plateau Mountains: Formed by erosion activity of rivers cutting over plateaus for billions of years. The Catskills Mountain in New York is a plateau mountain.

Are deserts always hot and covered with sand?

No, not all deserts are hot or covered with sand! It is common to imagine deserts with never-ending dunes of sand and cacti plants. The Gobi Desert in Asia and the extremely cold desert in Antarctica filled with acres of snow are good examples of cold deserts. Only 10 percent of all deserts on Earth are covered with sand.

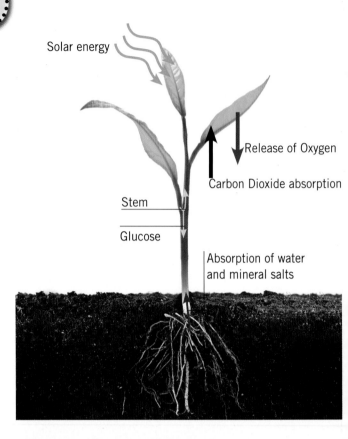

Solar energy

Release of Oxygen

Carbon Dioxide absorption

Stem

Glucose

Absorption of water and mineral salts

What is photosynthesis?

It is a process by which plants and some algae manufacture their own food using the carbon dioxide available in the atmosphere and sunlight. It is this special ability which puts the plants and other autotrophs at the very top of the food cycle. Most living things, including us, depend on these plants for our survival!

Do all plants depend only on photosynthesis for growing?

No, the carnivorous plants are a special category of plants that feed on insects. That's right - these plants capture insects through different interesting and novel mechanisms and digest them to get nitrogen compounds that are not available in the soil they grow in! There are two kinds of carnivorous plants – active and passive. The

What is special about Conifers?

Conifers hold a lot of records making them very unique in the Plant kingdom!

- One of the world's oldest trees is the Great Basin bristlecone pine of California and Nevada which is almost 5000 years old!

- The world's smallest trees are also conifers! The natural bonsai cypress and shore pines grow only to heights of about 20 cm.

- The world's tallest tree, the redwood is a conifer.

- The world's most massive tree, the giant sequoia is also a conifer!

- The world's fastest growing tree, the pine, is again a conifer. It can reach its full height in less than 20 years.

active plant type has a mechanism that closes the leaf trap after an insect enters and the passive type have a 'pitfall' mechanism in which the unlucky insect falls into a pitcher or jar-like structure and gets digested. The pitcher plant is a classic example of carnivorous or hunter plants.

What adaptations help plants survive in deserts?

Plants that live in deserts have some special adaptations that help them cope up with the extreme conditions. They have long roots that explore deep under the ground for water. They have waxy coating on their stems that prevent water loss. Plants like cacti have leaves modified into spines and store water in their stems.

How do the tiny insects protect themselves?

Insects might be tiny but they are masters of deception. Take the leaf litter mantis for instance – it can imitate a dead leaf to escape from predators and also disguise itself when hunting small insects! The stick insect can look strikingly like a twig that predators miss them completely. The saw-nosed plant hopper has big red spots on its wings that look like eyes – this helps the insect scare away faint-hearted predators! There are other insects like Hyalymenus Nymph that imitate the fierce sap-eating red ants. Even butterflies are good at deceiving predators by imitating their non-tasty cousins!

What are marsupials?

Marsupials are animals that carry their young ones in a special pouch designed for that purpose. Koalas, kangaroos, wallabies and opossums are some examples of marsupials. Virtually all species of marsupials are found in Australia and some in New Guinea.

Which are the smallest and biggest birds?

The bee humming bird is the smallest bird on Earth. The ostrich is the largest bird that cannot fly. Who wants wings when you can race at speeds of 40 miles per hour! The Andean condor happens to be the largest bird that can fly. They weigh up to 33 lbs and have a ten foot wing span!

Which mammal is considered closest to humans in terms of intelligence?

The chimpanzee is closest to us in terms of intelligence! For instance, chimps can make simple tools using sticks and stones. Some chimpanzees have even been thought to use sign language just like we do!

31

What are plankton?

Plankton are the tiny organisms found drifting along in the oceans. In fact, the name 'plankton' is a Greek word that means 'wanderer'! There are plant as well as animal plankton in the oceans and they are important sources of food and energy for the ecosystem. These tiny plankton are capable of blooming in large numbers so that they appear to change the colour of the ocean itself!

What are coral reefs?

Coral reefs are colourful communities of jellyfish-like organisms attached to limestone deposits in the ocean floor. Here is some surprising news – the coral is actually transparent and the spectacular colour of the coral reefs are due to the millions colourful of algae that attach to them!

Which are the largest and fastest creatures found in oceans?

The blue whale is the largest animal on the Earth. A blue whale calf weighs about two tons at birth!

The fastest creature in the ocean is thought to be the sailfish which can cruise across the ocean at speeds of 68 miles per hour.

Are there any fish that can live without water?

Amazing yet true – a type of fish called the mangrove rivulus live in logs when water dries up! Scientists have discovered that it can live out of water for up to 66 days!

What special organs do sharks have to detect prey?

Sharks are master hunters in the ocean because of their super-sharp senses! Two-thirds of a shark's brain is dedicated exclusively for its sense of smell. Sharks have mirror-like layer on their eyes that help them see better underwater. If that isn't enough, they have sensory organs that can detect vibrations or electric fields of their prey.

How have dolphins helped humans?

Dolphins are extremely intelligent creatures and for several years, incidents of dolphins forming a protective ring to rescue people from sharks have been recorded. Scientists believe that dolphins have the natural instinct to protect their young ones by nudging them along and they use the same procedure to help humans.

How does an oil spill affect aquatic life?

Even a small amount of oil spilt in the ocean can have a drastic effect on marine life. Fish, sea mammals, birds and marine life are affected in different ways. Oil coats the surface of these creatures and destroys their natural insulation and waterproofing properties! Their internal organs can be damaged if the oil is ingested. Oil can also affect coral reefs and sea grasses in the sea that provide food, shelter and living space to many aquatic species. Did you know that even an oil spill on land can sometimes find its way into lakes or oceans and affect marine life!

WORLD OF MICROBES

How did we know about microbes if they cannot be seen?

Anton van Leeuwenhoek has the privilege of being one of the first people to discover bacteria as early as in the 17th century. By the 19th century, scientists correlated that microbes were responsible for many diseases that affect us. Today we have many advanced microscopes that can magnify microbes several thousand fold!

What are the different types of microbes?

There are 6 major types of microbes: Archaea are single-celled organisms and come in different shapes. Bacteria are also single-celled and are known to inhabit virtually every place on Earth. Fungi can be single-celled or multi-celled. The best example of fungi is yeast that helps us in making bread. Viruses are microbes that can multiply inside a host, but outside the host it is inert and non-living. Protists include algae, slime molds, water molds and protozoa. Amoeba is a type of protozoa!

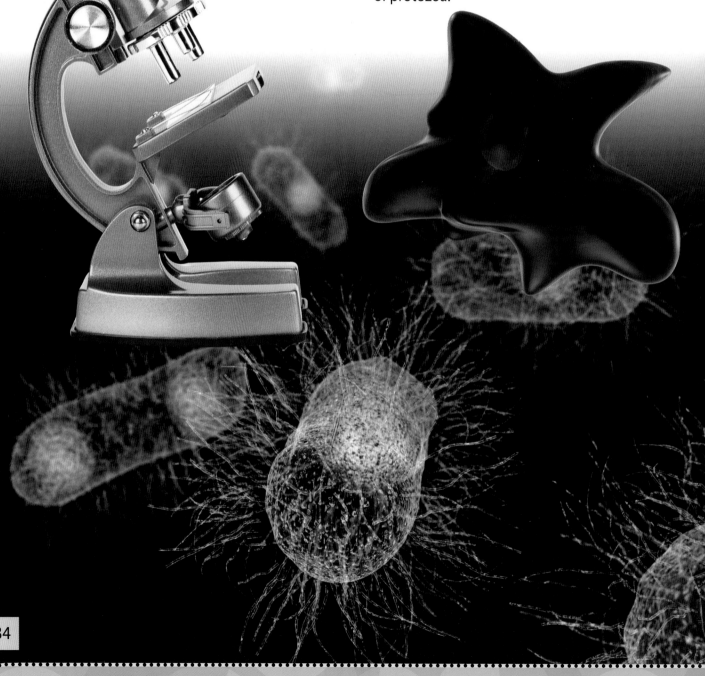

Which is the largest bacteria discovered on Earth?

Imagine being able to see a bacterium without using a microscope! The bacterium – Thiomargarita namibiensis is huge by bacterial standards with volume 3 million times greater than the average bacterium. It has a size of about 0.75 mm. They are not just big, they are very useful too! They remove poisonous sulphide compounds in the oceans which would otherwise accumulate and cause fish and other marine life to die.

Are microorganisms always harmful?

Definitely not! While many bacteria, virus and protozoa cause different diseases, not all microbes are bad or harmful. Many types of bacteria live inside and on the surface of our body without causing any disease. Many microbes like bacteria and fungi are even used in industrial production of acids, vitamins, pharmaceuticals, bio-fuels, dairy products, antibiotics and lots more.

Are there any microorganisms that survive in extreme conditions?

The microbes in the Archaea family live in extreme environments like ocean depths, sulphur lakes, thermal vents, geysers, petroleum deposits, salt water, and marshes in which no other living organism can survive! One of the first places where Archaea were first discovered is the Yellowstone National Park!

In what way does a virus differ from the other types of microorganisms?

When is a living thing not living? When it is a virus! Viruses are not living cells and have this unique capability to multiply within organisms but outside their hosts, viruses cannot live and exist as non-living things.

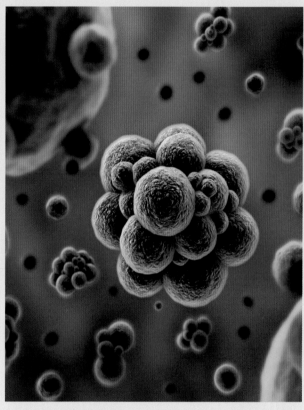

WEATHER AND CLIMATE

Is weather and climate the same?

While weather is how the conditions in the atmosphere behave over a short time, climate refers to events that happen in the atmosphere over a long time. You can know what the weather is like by listening to forecasts on television. Weather can change in a matter of minutes but climate takes several years, sometimes millions of years, to change.

- Aneroid Barometer: Measures atmospheric pressure

- Anemometer: Measures wind speeds

- Rain gauge: Measures amount of rainfall

- Thermometer: Measures temperature

- Psychrometer: Measures humidity or the amount of moisture in air

What are some common tools used in weather forecasting?

Meteorologists – people who study weather and climate – use many tools to provide you weather forecasts and disaster warnings. Here are some of them:

- Weather Satellite: It monitors the whole world from the top! It collects information like cloud patterns and hurricane formations. It has two sensors – one to read temperatures and the other to capture images.

- Doppler radar: It measures sound waves to identify precipitation and track storms

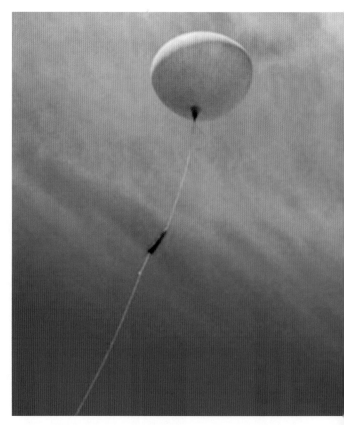

Does the moon have anything to do with the Earth's climate?

Moon definitely has a part to play in Earth's climate patterns! The moon exerts a gravitational pull on the Earth, causing the ocean tides to rise and fall. This affects the ocean currents which in turn bring about new temperature and weather patterns on the mainland. Also it has been noted that the Polar Regions are 0.55 °C warmer during a full moon!

What is the greenhouse effect?

If you have entered a greenhouse where plants are grown, you'll know how warm it is inside! Similarly, in the atmosphere there are many gases that hold on to the heat from the Sun, not allowing it to escape out. This will gradually cause the Earth to become much warmer. Burning fuels and cutting down trees will cause carbon dioxide (which is a greenhouse gas) to be released into the atmosphere thus enhancing the greenhouse effect!

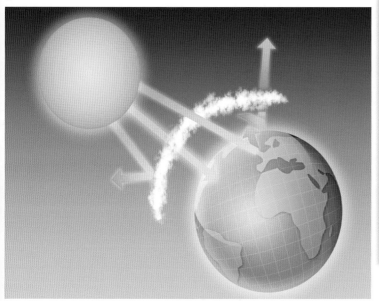

Is there any force acting against the greenhouse effect?

The mighty oceans that dominate the Earth apply a cooling effect on the climate by absorbing a lot of the carbon dioxide emitted. This in a way counteracts the greenhouse effect! But scientists do not know how long it will last!

What are the hottest and coldest temperatures recorded on Earth?

The hottest temperature recorded on Earth is 57.8 °C in Aziziya, Libya. The coldest temperature was recorded at the Vostok station in Antarctica which was -89.2 °C!

Natural Disasters

What are the types of natural disasters?

Any natural phenomena that occur unexpectedly and result in wide-scale destruction of lives and property are referred to as natural disasters. Some of the common natural disasters include earthquakes, volcanic eruptions, lightning, flood, tsunami, droughts, avalanches, landslides, blizzards, tornados, hurricanes and wildfires. Disease is also sometimes considered as a natural disaster.

What is a tsunami?

Tsunami refers to a series of ocean waves reaching heights of over 100 feet that send floods of water onto land. When these walls of water crash onto land, they can cause widespread destruction. It has been identified that tsunamis are caused by undersea earthquakes at tectonic plate boundaries, underwater landslides or volcanic eruptions. The tsunamis can travel across the sea at speeds of 500 miles per hour, which is about as fast as a jet plane!

How is an avalanche formed?

An avalanche is a formless mass of powdery snow that slides downhill, gaining more mass and speed. It is most likely to occur within 24 hours of a snowstorm that deposits more than 12 inches of snow. The occurrence of an avalanche depends on a lot of factors like temperature, wind, steepness of slope, storminess, orientation of terrain and vegetation. Avalanches can reach speeds of 80 miles per hour within five seconds. Around 150 people are killed in a year, worldwide, because of avalanches.

What is a tornado?

A tornado is a vertical funnel of spinning air that is created from huge, persistent thunderstorms. The wind speed of tornadoes can be 250 miles per hour. Tornadoes occur all over the world but USA is considered to be a hotspot of tornadoes and experiences more than 1000 a year! The common warning signs of tornadoes are dark and greenish sky, hail and roaring winds. The funnel of a tornado is usually transparent but it becomes visible when it absorbs water droplets, dust or debris.

What is drought?

A drought refers to a condition of prolonged dryness and lack of vegetation caused by decreased precipitation. Droughts can occur in all climatic zones and some of the factors responsible for droughts are high temperatures, high winds and low humidity apart from a deficiency in precipitation. It can severely affect agriculture and ecosystems and in extreme cases, the survival of living beings.

Can lightning be dangerous?

Of course! Lightning or bolts of electric discharge, caused by an imbalance of positive and negative charges during a storm, can be very dangerous and are known to kill around 2000 people a year worldwide! During a storm, colliding particles of rain droplets or ice gain negative charge while buildings, trees or persons become positively charged – this imbalance in charges is rectified by passing current between the two charges which occurs as lightning. Lightning bolts are extremely hot and can reach temperatures five times that of the Sun's surface! One lightning bolt contains a power of one billion volts of electricity.

How do blizzards affect us?

Blizzards are winter storms that cause severe wind and snow, exceeding speeds of 35 mph and that reduce visibility to less than ¼ of a mile for more than 3 hours and reduce temperature drastically. Driving becomes difficult or impossible during blizzards and the extreme cold temperatures can result in hypothermia or frostbite which can be life-threatening. The Great Blizzard of 1888 in eastern USA resulted in a death toll exceeding 400.

How can volcanic eruptions prove disastrous?

Large volcanic eruptions can be very dangerous for people living in close vicinity. The lava which flows from the volcano can have a temperature around 2000 °C! It has been estimated that more than 26,000 people have died in the past 300 years due to volcanic eruptions. Volcanoes erupt when magma, rocks, ash and toxic gases are forcefully expelled out of vents on the Earth's surface.

DIGGING OUT EVIDENCE

What does an archaeologist do?

An archaeologist is someone who tries to figure out what life was like in the ancient past by looking at the remains of ancient people through their fossils and their artifacts in archaeological sites.

Who studies dinosaurs and other prehistoric life?

While archaeologists focus only on learning about people who lived in the past, paleontologists are those who look for bones and remains of microbes, animals or birds and assemble them to find out more about it.

What are the tools that archaeologists and paleontologists generally use?

A wide range of tools like drills, trowels, chisels, picks and brushes are used for excavating the fossils from buried locations. It is then cleaned using toothpicks and specially-designed soft brushes. Microscopes are used to examine samples in greater detail.

What is an archaeological site?

A "site" is a place where archaeologists want to explore. At any archaeological site, archaeologists literally dig and look for the remains of an ancient civilization. A site can either be as small as a pile of chipped stone tools left by a prehistoric hunter who paused to sharpen a spear point, or as large and complex as the prehistoric settlements or towns, or Stonehenge in England.

Do archaeologists just choose a random spot to dig?

No! An archaeologist needs to find a specific place that looks promising for excavation. This is done by surveying different areas to see if there are any artifacts lying around. Sometimes computer-controlled instruments are used to look under the ground and decide whether a place is worth digging! For an archaeologist to find a site to explore takes a lot of time, work and planning. Archaeologists think about what resources people needed to stay alive, so it comes as no surprise to learn that archaeologists look for remains of civilizations along rivers and streams!

What is an artifact?

An artifact is the remains of something that was made in previous centuries by humans. In archaeology, where the term is most commonly used, an artifact is an object that was unearthed and recovered by some archaeologists with a cultural interest in mind like the bronze figure from the Indus valley civilization in India or the remains from the ancient Etruscan civilization in Italy.

What are fossils?

Fossils are evidence of ancient life that is preserved in sedimentary rocks, amber or other such material. Fossils act like clues that point us to what living things, ecosystems and environments were like in the past! The oldest fossils of bacteria that lived about 3.4 billion years ago, have been found preserved between quartz sand grains in Earth's oldest rock formations in Australia. The youngest fossils are from animals that lived before the beginning of recorded history, about 10,000 years ago.

What are some of the famous archaeological sites?

Among the various archaeologist sites that have been discovered, some of the famous ones include:

- Maachu Picchu in Peru
- The Great Pyramids of Egypt
- Easter Island statues of Polynesia
- Angkor Wat of Cambodia
- Pompeii in Italy
- Stonehenge in England
- Petra in Jordan

DINOSAURS

What does the word dinosaur mean?

The word dinosaur means 'terrible lizard'. The term was coined by Sir Richard Owen, a popular paleontologist of his time. The different species of dinosaurs were usually given binomial names by the scientific groups involved in finding and researching them.

What was the time period when dinosaurs lived called?

The Dinosaurs lived during the Mesozoic Era which is roughly 250 million years to 65 million years ago. The Mesozoic Era is in turn divided into the Triassic period, the Jurassic period and the Cretaceous period. The Jurassic period was the most significant period of dinosaur domination on Earth – large and fierce dinosaurs roamed about on Earth during this time! It is believed that dinosaurs evolved soon after a mass extinction event that happened in the Permian period.

How do dinosaur bones remain intact after millions of years?

We know so much about dinosaurs and other animals and birds that lived millions of years ago, thanks to the process called fossilization. It is lengthy and rare process that happens only under certain conditions. When a dinosaur dies, its body gets decomposed and only the bones remain. Layers of sediment accumulate above these bones and the pressure increases over years. This results in the formation of sedimentary rock in which dinosaur bones are preserved intact. The flow of mineral-rich water through the sedimentary rock also results in replacement of calcium in the bones with minerals making them much stronger and more likely to be preserved!

Did all dinosaurs hunt and eat animals?

No! There were different types of dinosaurs and only some ate other animals. Large and spectacular-looking dinosaurs like Brachiosaurus, Diplodocus and Triceratops were herbivores! Other dinosaurs were scavengers – and they ate the remains of animals already killed by other carnivorous animals.

Where did the dinosaurs live on Earth?

About 230 million years back, in the Triassic Period, there were no continents like today. Instead there was a single supercontinent called Pangaea that eventually broke apart into individual continents. Paleontologists have evidence that dinosaurs lived in all the continents that now exist!

Were all dinosaurs large?

Not all dinosaurs grew to monstrous heights. The height, body nature and adaptations of dinosaurs varied based on its eating habits and defence. Scientists believe that conifer trees dominated at the time and some dinosaurs evolved to be huge in order to reach great heights for leaves. Similarly, dinosaurs were equipped with powerful claws, teeth and stature to help them hunt better. That said, there were dinosaurs even as small as a chicken! The Compsognathus dinosaur is considered to be the smallest with a total length of about 70 centimetres – and that includes its tail too!

Did birds evolve from dinosaurs?

For long, scientists have thought that birds are related to dinosaurs. Birds and dinosaurs share some common features like scaly feet, shelled eggs and skeleton structure. The Archaeopteryx which was capable of flight and the Compsognathus were similar to birds in many ways and add credit to the theory that birds evolved from dinosaurs.

Were dinosaurs able to make any sound?

It is difficult to find out whether dinosaurs made any sound based only on their fossils. But scientists have identified hollow bony channels that connected to the nasal passages in certain fossils! What does this mean? This could mean that when the dinosaurs exhaled, they produced sounds that could be anything from trumpeting to hissing!

Did any dinosaurs live in the sea?

Based on all fossil evidences discovered so far, there are no known aquatic dinosaurs. There were aquatic creatures like Plesiosaurs and Ichthyosaurs that existed at about the same time as dinosaurs but they lacked features present in the common ancestors of dinosaur. Many dinosaurs were known to live along the coasts, but were not necessarily aquatic.

What makes Tyrannosaurus Rex one of the fiercest dinosaurs?

The Tyrannosaurus Rex had extremely powerful jaws and about 60 teeth, each about 20 centimetres long! The name actually means 'King of the Cruel Rulers'. Fossil evidence shows that this dinosaur could bite right through bones, and its bite is supposed to be about 3 times more powerful than a lion's!

What is the

Coelophysis?

The Coelophysis was a dinosaur which had hollow bones similar to those of birds. These dinosaurs were about the size of turkeys and were very swift and agile. They had long necks, tails and legs. They were believed to have fed on insects, lizard-like reptiles and even small dinosaurs!

Why did Stegosaurus have an armoured body and tail?

Stegosaurus was a herbivore that is well-known for the rows of large bony plates lining its body and tail. It used its powerful tail to lash out at predators and defend itself. Scientists believe that its body plates might have protected it from predator attack, helped regulate its body temperature or even helped members of the same species identify each other!

What do we know about Diplodocus?

Diplodocus was about 90 feet long and lived in the Jurassic Era! This vegetarian dinosaur had a long flexible neck that allowed it to graze over a wide area without moving. These dinosaurs had stomach stones that helped with digestion. The long tail helped balance the body of Diplodocus when they walked.

What is unique about Triceratops?

Triceratops had one of the largest skulls among dinosaurs that lived on land! This dinosaur had a very large head that accommodated 3 horns, a large beak-like mouth and a frill that could grow to about 1 foot! The horns were used for protecting itself from predator attacks. Scientists believe that the frill might either have been used for protecting its neck or attracting mates. Despite its fierce and formidable appearance, Triceratops was a herbivore.

What special record does the Brachiosaurus hold?

The Brachiosaurus is thought to be one of the biggest, longest and heaviest dinosaurs of all time. Scientists believe that these dinosaurs must have had extremely powerful hearts capable of pumping blood all the way up their long necks to their brain! This plant-eating dinosaur must have required about 440 pound of food every day to keep it going!

Did Oviraptors steal eggs?

Oviraptor which means 'egg thief' might actually be an inaccurate name for these dinosaurs! The fossil of this dinosaur along with a batch of eggs was discovered in 1995. Initially it was thought that the eggs were robbed from the nest of another dinosaur species, thus giving it the name. But other fossils uncovered later show these dinosaurs in brooding position much similar to that of birds, making scientists believe that the fossilized dinosaur was protecting its own eggs!

What were the features that made Velociraptor a powerful hunter?

What an apt name for this intelligent dinosaur – Velociraptor means 'swift predator'. Velociraptor was a dinosaur that probably hunted in packs, as seen from fossil evidence. These dinosaurs were only about the size of a full-grown human but they had some special weaponry that made them deadly predators – they were incredibly quick with speeds of about 24 mph, had retractable 3.5 inch-long claws and a mouth filled with about 80 razor-sharp teeth!

Prehistoric Birds

What is a Dodo?

This flightless bird lived until about 300 years ago! It was found on Mauritius Island in the Indian Ocean. The Dodo bird was large and resembled a turkey but is believed to be related to pigeons. The clumsy and slow-moving birds got hunted for meat by Dutch settlers as well as the animals like monkeys, cats, rats and hogs introduced by the settlers. The last Dodo bird was seen in 1681!

Were there any other birds like Dodo living at that time?

The Solitaires were birds related to the Dodo and were found in the nearby islands – Rodriguez and Runion. Sadly, this bird species outlived the Dodo only by a few hundred years and became extinct in the 1800's.

Which is the largest bird known to us?

The aptly named Terror Bird might not have been able to fly, but it was one of the biggest birds we have ever known! Scientists say that these birds were so powerful that they could have swallowed prey, the size of a dog, easily in one gulp! Not really difficult with a beak about 18 inches (or about 46 centimetres) long! That's not all – these birds were believed to have been about 10 feet tall and had a skull about two-and-half feet long and could have killed its prey with one blow!

What is a Moa?

The Moa was another type of flightless bird that was anything from 3 to 13 feet tall and found in New Zealand in the 1400's. Scientists believe that a few existed until the 1600's before they were completely wiped out. Though the reason for their extinction is unclear, it is thought that the Maori tribal people who were the earliest inhabitants of New Zealand hunted the birds to extinction.

Which was the largest flying bird that lived on Earth?

The Pelagornis which had gigantic wings that spanned about 17 feet was one of the largest flying birds ever known. These birds were found on Earth about 5 to 10 million years ago and must have looked really scary with their jagged beaks and hollow spikes on their beaks which would have helped them grip their prey.

What is an Elephant Bird?

Also known as Aepyornis, this flightless bird was found in Madagascar and is thought to have become extinct 500 to 700 years ago. With a height of about 10 feet and weighing about 1000 pounds, the Elephant bird is one of the heaviest birds we have ever known and laid gigantic eggs. Do you know the size of one egg? About 34 centimetres!

Are there any extinct water birds we know of?

The fossils of Gansus, a type of aquatic bird, were found in regions surrounding rivers and lakes in Asia. They were thought to have lived in the early Cretaceous period, about 110 million years ago. This bird is thought to have behaved like a modern duck because it was well-adapted for diving underneath water for fish.

Which was the earliest known bird which is extinct now?

The Archaeopteryx which lived about 150 million years ago is the earliest known bird and is said to have been about the size of a crow! It had toothed jaws and a tail too, making it look more like a reptile! This bird had special feet that helped it climb trees and perch comfortably on branches.

Did any sea creatures like dinosaurs exist?

Much like the mythical Loch Ness monster in appearance, Plesiosaurs were creatures that inhabited the sea about 200 million years ago at the about the same time as dinosaurs. They were 20 to 23 feet in length and had a very long neck, small head and a huge body!

What were the ammonites?

Ammonites were sea creatures that lived at the same time as the dinosaurs. This animal had no spinal column, but was protected by a shell that was made out of calcium. This animal ate other small sea animals and was known for its great speed as well. They came in different sizes ranging from one inch to about 3 metres in diameter. They are most closely related to octopuses and squid.

Were there any snake-like creatures back then?

Mosasaurs were reptiles that closely resembled monitor lizards and snakes! They lived about 80 to 90 million years ago and would have eaten turtles, fish and mollusks. They had very strong teeth that they used for crushing shelled animals before consuming them. They would have spent most of their time in water and would have swum like a snake with the help of their finned tail.

Were there any amphibians during the time of the dinosaurs?

The Gerrothorax is a great example of prehistoric amphibians. This creature was about one metre long and lived about 200 million years ago during the Triassic era. It had a flattened body and looked more or less like a large tadpole. But what makes it much different from a tadpole is the presence of dozens of sharp, fang-like teeth to attack its prey! It had a wide and short head, two close-set eyes and a small tail. It also had three pairs of gills that helped it live under water.

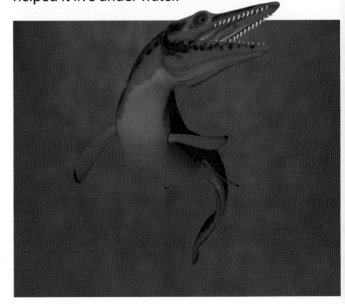

What was considered to be the fiercest creature in the sea?

A species of bony fish called Xiphactinus is considered to be one of the fiercest sea creatures of prehistoric times! This monster of a fish was about 17 feet long and had powerful tail, wing-like fins and sharp fang-like teeth. The upturned jaw structure of this fish gave it the appearance of a bulldog!

Were there any prehistoric creatures that existed before the dinosaurs?

The Trilobite was a hard-shelled marine animal similar to a crab that lived around 520 million years ago, and went extinct before the dinosaurs evolved. Scientists have described more than 20000 species of Trilobites, now signature creatures of the Paleozoic Era. Some Trilobites were versatile – some were plant-eaters, a few were scavengers, while still others ate decayed materials.

Were there any prehistoric frogs?

Scientists have found a prehistoric species of frog called the Devil Frog, which weighed about 10 lbs and grew up to 16 inches. It is supposed to be the largest frog ever known - about the size of a beach ball. These monster frogs were not only large but also very aggressive! Their diet included lizards, small animals and even newly-hatched dinosaurs!

Did prehistoric giant sharks exist?

The Megalodon was an ancient shark that might have lived 25 million years ago. It was known to have been around 12m long. Fossil studies reveal that these sharks must have had teeth as big as a human hand! No other part of this ancient shark has been found, but by studying its teeth, we speculate that it might have eaten whales as its prey.

EXTINCTION!

When did the dinosaurs become extinct?

There are so many theories that explain how dinosaurs became extinct. Among these, there is one where dinosaurs became extinct about 65 million years ago as a result of the after-effects of an asteroid impact! And the proof? A huge crater found in Yucatan Peninsula near Mexico dated to be about 65 million years old, exactly coinciding with their extinction!

Is it true that dinosaurs were wiped out when an asteroid hit Earth?

The most popular theory about dinosaur extinction is the Asteroid theory. According to this theory, it is believed that a large asteroid or comet collided with the Earth about 65 million years ago. Paleontologists and scientists believe that such a large scale collision resulted in heavy dust that would have prevented sunlight from entering the earth and that would have led to plants and animals, including dinosaurs, to die because of the lack of sunlight and vegetation.

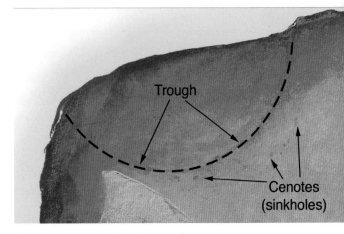

Trough

Cenotes (sinkholes)

When was the first dinosaur ever found?

Although there are suggestions that people have been unearthing and finding dinosaur fossils for hundreds of years, the earliest references to "dragon bones" were from Wucheng, Sichuan in China. It was written down by a person called Chang Qu over 2,000 years ago and he was probably referring to dinosaur fossils!

However, the first dinosaur to be described scientifically was the Megalosaurus in 1824 by William Buckland after he discovered its fossil in 1819.

What was the oldest dinosaur ever found?

Researchers are unearthing new evidence all the time and it is difficult to pinpoint the oldest dinosaur ever discovered. According to the most recent studies, footprints of a dinosaur, which has been named Protodactylus, and which lived about 250 million years ago, have been discovered in Poland. These dinosaurs were hardly bigger than a cat!

How many dinosaurs were there ?

It is difficult to come up with an exact figure, but scientists have estimated that there must have been at least 1844 genera of dinosaurs and only a small percent (about 29%) have been discovered so far. Let us hope we uncover more interesting and exciting dinosaurs in the future!

Could the Ice Age have caused dinosaur extinction?

Scientists believe that the Earth has undergone several ice ages. For example, during the last ice age which ended about 10,000 years ago, the climate would have been so severe that it could have drastically changed temperatures and frozen a lot of the Earth's water. The dinosaurs when exposed to such temperatures would not have been able to cope with such extreme conditions, thus leading to their mass extinction.

Is there any other theory about how dinosaurs could have gone extinct?

Another theory of dinosaur extinction that has been suggested by scientists, is volcanic activity. Scientists believe that a huge increase in volcanic activity happened around 65 million years ago which could have pumped so much ash into the air that it blocked out the sunlight, caused global temperatures to fall and led to the mass extinction of the dinosaurs.

PREHISTORIC HUMANS

Did early humans live at the same time as dinosaurs?

No, early humans did not exist in the time period when dinosaurs existed. Dinosaurs ruled the Earth in the Mesozoic Era and became extinct about 65 million years before humans evolved. The first hominids or human-like primates surfaced on the earth only about 3.6 million years ago.

When did humans first appear?

Scientists do not really know when exactly humans appeared on Earth but an analysis of bones, artifacts and other material provides some clues. Somewhere in the middle of the Stone Age, about 73,000 B.C., a huge volcanic eruption occurred. This was considered the biggest volcanic eruption to have occurred in the last 2 million years! The volcanic ash in the atmosphere caused the temperatures to drop drastically. Scientists believe that this must have caused most of the hominids to be wiped out leaving behind a small population. Humans are believed to have evolved from this population, eventually leading to us!

Who was the Homo habilis?

The Homo habilis species of humans were fondly referred to as 'handy man' by scientists owing to the different tools that have been discovered along with their fossils. These humans evolved about 2.3 million years ago and they realized that in order to survive, they needed weapons to help them fight, so they invented tools to help live more comfortably and protect themselves against carnivores. Scientists believe that this species might have developed the ability to communicate through simple speech.

What was Homo erectus?

About 1.8 million years ago, Homo habilis evolved into Homo erectus or the "Upright Man" and were about the same size as the modern human, but only had two thirds of our brain capacity. The basic tool-making skills had improved and tools produced included axes and knives. It is widely thought that they were probably the first hunters and fire-makers!

Who were the Neanderthal humans?

Neanderthal humans evolved 250,000 years ago and are thought to have lived in very cold climates. They had thick bones and muscular bodies needed to survive the cold, harsh climate. They had a brain slightly larger than the average humans have today and lived in Europe and Middle East regions. About 20 different tools used by Neanderthals have been identified and could have been used for a variety of purposes like cutting wood, slicing meat and scraping hides.

When and where did the modern humans emerge?

You and all other human beings you see today belong to the species Homo sapiens that appeared about 190,000 years ago in Africa! What made them unique from the other species was the large brain, prominent chin, small eyebrow ridges, forehead that rises sharply and lighter bone structure. They built shelters, hunted for food and lived together in groups.

How did they differ from the earlier species?

About 40,000 years ago, Homo sapiens started becoming really creative and artistic! They started making advanced tools like spears, bow and arrows, harpoons and sewing needles with different materials such as bone and antler! What's more, in the following 20,000 years they started producing cave paintings, carvings in ivory, clay figurines and even musical instruments.

Are there people now who closely resemble ancient humans?

The San people of Africa, who are commonly called 'Bushmen', are hunters and gatherers who show more resemblance to the early humans than any other group of people on earth. Even the language they use to communicate, called Xu, has a lot of clicking sounds similar to how our ancestors might have communicated!

CIVILIZATIONS

When did civilizations start to form?

When humans began to develop a more complex way of life, they began to live in towns and cities that increased in size and were more complex to rule, thus leading to the emergence of a more complex society, known as a civilization. People in a civilization share a common culture, common laws, common economy, and in most cases a common faith or religion.

What does cultural identity mean?

Cultural identity is a term that is used for describing a set of ideas, customs, arts and religion that make a certain society or civilization unique. Civilizations often develop a complicated culture, which can   also include language, literature, professional art, architecture, religion, and other complex customs.

When did people start doing specific jobs?

After the prehistoric era, humans continued to do whatever they could to find food and shelter for themselves and their families like hunting, dressing, food gathering and making tools. However, as societies became larger, certain individuals became much better than others at doing certain things, which made them specialize in different types of jobs. It became clear that it was no longer necessary for one individual to do every kind of job, instead one person could specialize at making pottery, for example, and another at making tools!

When did the trade routes develop?

As civilizations grew and societies became more advanced, the demand for certain products like tin and copper increased. People also began to want products that were not readily available in their own lands, such as exotic spices, grains and animals. This was when the trade routes started to develop. At first the routes were quite simple, but with the passage of time the routes became more complex and specialized traders, known as merchants traded goods from one society to another, sometimes travelling long distances.

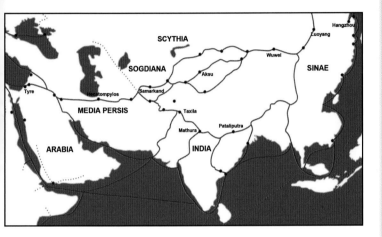

Where was the earliest civilization found?

One of the earliest civilizations to develop also happens to be one of the most famous civilizations in the world! This civilization grew out of the people who inhabited the valley along Africa's Nile River. The river Nile provided an endless source of fresh water, soil and food.

When was written language developed?

As culture became more complex, the spoken word was not enough; hence people needed to keep records about what was going on in their societies. Did you know that the first people who began to record in writing were priests! They recorded names of those who had donated religious offerings. Traders also began recording what they had bought and sold, and leaders recorded laws for their people to learn and follow.

What were the seven wonders of the ancient world?

The seven wonders of the ancient world were built between 3000 B.C. and 476 A.D. and included these structures:

- The Great Pyramids of Giza

- The Lighthouse of Alexandria

- The Hanging Gardens of Babylon

- Temple of Zeus

- The Colossus of Rhodes

- The Temple of Artemis

- The Mausoleum of Halicarnassus

Of the seven ancient wonders, only the Great Pyramids of Giza exist today. Scholars even doubt if the hanging gardens actually existed!

ANCIENT EGYPT

When did the first settlements in the Nile Valley begin?

The first settlements in the Nile Valley began around 7,000 years ago. Like other parts of the world, these prehistoric settlements slowly developed into more complex societies. The first people who inhabited this region called their land 'kemet', which means 'black lands'. They gave it this name because of the rich black soil that was found there!

What were the Egyptian Pyramids?

Egyptian people in ancient times believed that their rulers were gods. They believed that after their deaths, these rulers would continue to work on behalf of the Egyptian nation, so they made a lot of efforts to honour their dead rulers, so much so that they would bury them with elaborate treasures, food and even servants. The remains of the dead rulers were laid to rest in elaborate burial chambers in large stone buildings known as pyramids that stretched up towards the sky. These pyramids took decades and hundreds of thousands of labourers to construct.

What was the old kingdom in ancient Egypt?

With the evolution of societies, it led to a situation where people needed a class of people to rule over the society. That was why the old Kingdom in Egypt came into being. Egyptian rulers at the time grew in power and influence, to the point that people began to consider them not only as kings, but also as Gods.

What is a mummy?

The bodies of the Egyptian kings and pharaohs as well as those of other important individuals were preserved from decay through the process of mummification where the body is ceremonially preserved by removing the internal organs and treating the body with natron, resin and wrapping it in bandages. The first part of the procedure where the body is cleansed and preserved is called 'embalming'. The second part in which bandages are wrapped around the preserved body is called 'wrapping'.

What was the Middle kingdom in Egypt?

For over four centuries Egypt enjoyed peace and prosperity, but in 2200 B.C. there started a series of civil wars when local leaders rose in rebellion, and this lasted 150 years. It was around 2050 B.C. that a new king united Egypt once again.

What was the new Kingdom in Egypt?

In 1700 B.C. another war arose from another threat - that of an invasion by a desert people known as Hyksos. Using superior weapons and technology, the Hyksos conquered the Egyptians, and ruled them for the next century. However, the Egyptians eventually overthrew them, thus beginning the period known as the New Kingdom. The kings of the New kingdom were the first to be referred to as Pharaohs.

When did the Egyptian empire begin to decline?

In 1100 B.C. the pharaoh by the name of Ramses III led Egypt into a war in an attempt to conquer Syria. This war was a costly one and drained the treasury of Egypt. This began the decline of a once powerful and majestic kingdom.

What did the ancient Egyptians eat?

As Egypt was very dry, and relied mostly on the river Nile to water the crops, people could only grow wheat and barley. The ancient Egyptians were also date and meat eaters.

What kinds of weapons did the ancient Egyptians use?

The ancient Egyptians used a wide range of weapons including: spears, bows and arrows, cudgels or clubs, maces, daggers, battle axes, swords, catapults, razors, traps and boomerangs.

ANCIENT GREECE

Who ruled Greece before the Greeks?

Before the Greek civilization began, another great civilization flourished in the same region. These people where known as the Minoans and they flourished from around 2500 B.C. until about 1400 BC. It is believed that this civilization was both powerful and advanced. Some archeological finds have pointed that they had curled hair and wore gold jewelry.

Who were the ancient Greeks?

The ancient Greeks are believed to be the founders of the modern world. It is true that their culture existed thousands of years ago, but their ideas, building designs, sports and governments still exist in the Western World today.

How did the view of religion change with the Greeks?

Before the Greeks, religion was mostly based on fear where people believed in gods and goddesses that were terrible, mean and not human but animals, monsters, and beasts. The Greeks however had a new outlook on religion where they believed that the gods and mankind had a partnership with each other and believed that their gods were human in form, with the only difference between them and the gods was that the gods had supernatural powers. Each Greek city-state selected a patron god as their protector. This god was worshiped, so that their good favor would fall upon the people of that region. Every Greek Citizen also worshiped the chief god Zeus.

What was the Trojan horse?

The Greeks believed in two myths known as the Iliad and the Odyssey. Among the stories in these myths, there is one of a giant wooden horse. In the story, an army attempted to conquer the city of Troy after many years of failed attempts, they devise a plot. The soldiers of this army built a giant wooden horse, which they filled with their best and strongest soldiers. The Trojans, who thought that the army that built the horse had left, took the horse into their city. During the night, Greece's best soldiers climbed out of the horse and finally overthrew the city.

How did the Olympics come into being?

As the Greek civilization continued to evolve, they began to practice many important festivals. One of these festivals was a sporting event that took place every four years in the city of Olympia. These sporting events celebrated fitness and strength. Citizens of Greece would travel to Olympia from all over the nation to take part in a variety of sporting events where they could demonstrate their strength and athleticism.

Who were the Spartans?

Sparta was another city in ancient Greece that had a very different form of governing. They decided that the best way to ensure that their people remained obedient to their laws was to create a massive army, and all Spartan boys were expected to join the army. At birth, if a male child did not appear to be strong, officials would leave the baby on a hill to die. At the age of 7, a boy was required to leave their families and begin to train to become soldiers. They would remain in the army till they turned 60!

Who was Alexander the Great?

Alexander was a young Macedonian who was taught for four years, politics, war and critical thinking by Aristotle, one of the famous Greek philosophers. When Alexander was 20, his father was murdered, after which he became the king. After having been tutored by the philosopher, he admired the Greeks and their culture. He also admired the Persian culture and was convinced to conquer both places and combine both in an empire that could not be matched by any other in the world. For the next 13 years Alexander the Great marched his troops from battle to battle to conquer more and more territories.

ANCIENT ROME

Who were the Ancient Romans?

Rome when it started was just a small village, but with time it grew into the most powerful empire in the world. According to legend, Rome was founded by a young man by the name of Romulus. It is believed that he built a wall around his village and would kill anyone who ever tried to break the walls of Rome. However, most archaeologists and historians believed that Rome began as a series of small villages that were set around 7 hills. It is believed that these villages over time merged into a larger city that eventually became Rome.

How were the Romans governed?

The people of ancient Rome were governed by select members known as patricians. These leaders could be elected to the Senate, which was made up of 300 elected leaders. The senate voted on laws, authorized war, building projects, taxes and other matters of public interest. In addition to the senate, the Romans also elected two leaders to an office, which they called consuls. These consuls had a great deal of power when they acted together. However, they could not do anything alone. One consul had the authority to veto the decisions of the other, thus helping to keep the power of either in check.

What did the Early Romans believe in?

The ancient Romans did not invent a new religion of their own. They worshipped the same spirits worshiped by their former rulers and also began to worship the Greek gods and gave them new Roman names. For instance, Zeus became Jupiter, Aphrodite became Venus and so forth.

How were the Romans able to conquer and expand their empire?

The Romans faced threats on every side by other groups of people who lived on the Italian Peninsula, so in order to protect themselves, they began to develop a powerful military. All Roman citizens were required to serve in the military when needed, which somehow insured a constant available supply of soldiers and led them to be the undisputed ruling power of the Italian peninsula.

What was the Triumvirate?

After the death of Julius Caesar the Roman Empire was divided up and ruled by three of Caesar's former generals. These generals were Octavian, Marc Antony, and Marcus Lepidus. These three leaders formed what they called the Triumvirate. Each member of the triumvirate had absolute authority over matters that took place within their portion of the empire.

Who was Julius Caesar?

In 60 B.C. a young and ambitious general by the name of Julius Caesar stepped into political life. Caesar was very successful on the battlefield and had greatly expanded Rome's borders, so the senate was always afraid that he would overthrow the government, which eventually happened when he disobeyed the senate's order and a civil war erupted. In 45 B.C. he defeated opposing forces and took control over the Roman Empire.

Who was Augustus Caesar?

After Octavian Caesar was elected by the senate as a consul for life, he changed his name to Augustus, which means 'Majestic One'. Augustus Caesar ruled Rome from 27 B.C. until his death in 14 A.D.

What did the ancient Romans eat?

For breakfast, ancient Roman's ate salted bread, milk or wine, and perhaps dried fruit, eggs or cheese. Lunch included salted bread or was more elaborate with fruit, salad, eggs, meat or fish, vegetable, and cheese. Dinner was always accompanied by wine that was usually well-watered.

ANCIENT INDIA AND CHINA

Who were the Indus Valley people?

For many thousands of years, people have been living in the Indus River Valley. They were known as the Indus Valley civilization and they lived a simple life of hunting, gathering, and later, farming and agriculture. However they were known to be very organized and built a well defined drainage system and made jewelry and toys for children.

Who were the Aryans?

According to popular belief, the Indus Valley civilization was wiped out by a flood giving way to another civilization that was more technically advanced. These people were known as the Aryans. The Aryans were fair skinned people who used superior strength to conquer the people of the Indus River Valley.

What were the Vedas?

For many hundreds of years, the Aryans did not have a written language and passed their history down from one generation to another through stories, poems and epics. Around 1200 B.C. the Aryans developed a written language that was handed down and was recorded in sacred books called Vedas, or "Books of Knowledge". The Vedas gave historians an accurate picture into the lives and culture of the Aryan peoples.

Which period was known as the Golden Age of ancient Indian history?

India was ruled by a number of dynasties, of which the Gupta dynasty under the leadership of Chandragupta was well known. Under his rule, there was a period of great advances in art, science and philosophy, which is why this period is known as the 'Golden Age' of Indian history.

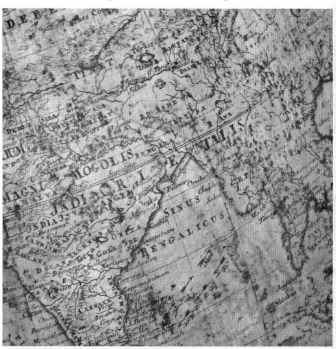

When did the Chinese civilization start?

The Chinese civilization, which is the oldest civilization that still exists today, goes back in history in an unbroken chain clearly covering over 4000 years. Throughout these years the Chinese people have been involved in developing technologies and advancing the knowledge of mankind. The Chinese have been ruled by a succession of dynasties.

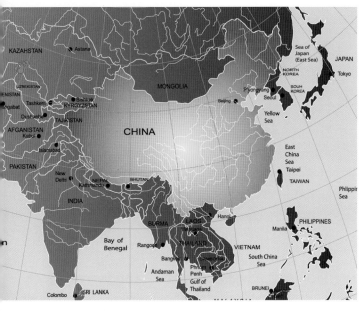

What was the Han dynasty?

In the year 207 B.C. a dynasty lead by a peasant named Liu Bang was formed. Liu Bang had grown tired of the brutal leadership of the previous Qin Dynasty and believed that the Qin dynasty had lost the right to rule the nation. With the backup of all the people, he was able to overthrow them and establish himself as the new emperor and his descendants ruled China for the next 400 years.

Why was the Great Wall of China constructed?

The early emperors of China had built walls in the northern parts to protect their nation against the attack from foreign forces. These walls were spread across the landscape, but were not connected. When the Qin dynasty came into place, the ambitious emperor Qin ordered his people to connect all the existing walls together and to expand them, eventually covering a distance of over 4000 miles. Over 300,000 peasants were forced to help build the Great Wall of China with many dying during construction. After working for

several years, the Great Wall of China was completed, and still stands today as one of the great building projects in human history.

What was the Silk route?

In order to make trade possible, the emperor Wudi from the Liang dynasty developed what has been called in modern times, the Silk Route. Following these routes, merchant traders brought silk from China to the West and glass, linen and gold from the West back to China. Did you know that this route consisted of trails, roads, bridges and pathways that stretched across nearly 5000 miles of land and water!

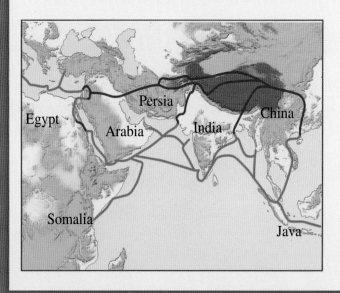

Ancient America

Who were the Mayans?

Around 2500 B.C. the Olmec tribe of South America flourished in the Yucatan peninsula, but around 4000 B.C. they were overthrown by another powerful tribe called the Mayans. Although no one knew where they came from, they arrived with amazing skills and were advanced and clever people. Soon enough, they overtook Yucatan Peninsula of central America.

What is a Stela?

Mayans built the 'stela' to celebrate the K'atun festival that was held every 20 years. A very large stone slab inscribed with hieroglyphics had inscriptions about the event. Stelas were always placed where people could see them and were designed with drawings so that people could understand them better.

How were the Mayan cities built?

The Mayans were master builders, but interestingly they did not use metal. Their tools were made of stone, wood, and shell. What is so remarkable is that even without metal tools, they were able to build huge cities with strong buildings and pyramids that were 200 feet high! Each Mayan city had a central marketplace, a large plaza where people could gather, huge pyramids, temples, at least one ball court and a palace for the city ruler. These cities were connected with extremely well built roads that ran for miles.

What were the Mayan pyramids?

The Mayans built two kinds of pyramids. One was designed to honour a god, while the other was for priests to conduct ceremonies, with the most important ceremonies being conducted at the top of the pyramids. Because these ceremonies were held at the top of the pyramids, Mayan pyramids had flat tops.

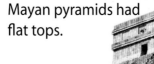

Why were the Mayan temples built?

Mayans built temples as sacred places of worship and home to the many priests and like the palaces, they had a central courtyard that offered privacy to those living there and at the foot of each temple they had their famous ball courts.

What kind of religion did the Mayans follow?

For the Mayans, worshipping their gods was a very vital part of their daily lives and they worshipped the gods of nature every day. Mayans also believed in the afterlife, with most of the common people burying the dead in their homes, but the nobles were buried in tombs. They also conducted many ceremonies to keep the demons, creatures and gods in the Underworld, where they belonged.

What did the Mayans invent?

The Maya invented some of the most advanced things for their time. They had a very advanced form of writing known as hieroglyphics (which is not related to the Egyptian hieroglyphics). Among their other inventions, the ancient Mayans invented a calendar that was complex, but had a remarkable accuracy. This calendar was adopted by others such as the Aztecs and the Toltec civilizations too.

What is a unique contribution of the Aztecs to the world?

Aztecs originally invented chocolate which was served as a celebratory beverage produced from fermented pulp of cacao beans! It is said the Aztec Emperor Montezuma consumed 50 cups of chocolate every day!

Who were the Incas?

The Incas were a tribe who lived in South America near the Andes Mountain range around 1250 A.D. By the 15th century they had built a huge empire by conquering many of the neighbouring kingdoms! The Incas were expert farmers – they cultivated many crops in terraced slopes and domesticated the llamas and alpacas for wool. The sacred city of the Incas was Cuzco which stood atop the Andes mountain of central Peru.

MEDIEVAL EUROPE

When did the medieval age begin?

With the collapse of the Roman Empire the overall situation in Europe worsened. There was less food, poorer education and miserable living conditions that were much worse than previous generations. This time period came to be known as the Dark Ages or Medieval times. Medieval means "Middle Age" and refers to the fact that these difficult times bridged the ancient world with the modern world.

What was the Little Ice Age?

Between the 14th and 19th centuries, Europe experience much harsher and colder climates than in the 20th century – it is this period which historians refer to as 'Little Ice Age' and crop failure and famines were common.

What kind of food did the people eat?

The type of cuisine varied greatly among the people. Kings, nobles and knights enjoyed royal feasts that included cooked meat of partridges, geese, larks, chickens and other birds, wheat bread, pastries and wine. But peasants and poor people were lucky if they got bread every day. The bread they ate was made of barley and rye. A type of beer, called ale, was a popular drink among the poor people.

What was the Black Death?

The Black Death refers to a contagious form of bubonic plague that raged from 1347 to 1351 in Europe. The plague was so called, because infected persons developed swellings that eventually turned black. It was caused by fleas carried by rats and rodents thought to have been brought from Asia by European traders. This plague epidemic killed about 1.5 million people in Europe!

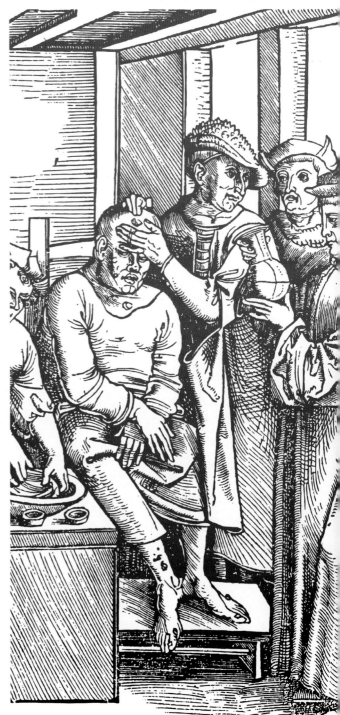

Who were the Vikings?

In 800 A.D. one of the Germanic warrior tribes whose homeland was Scandinavia decided to leave their homes in search of wealth and adventure because their native land had become too crowded. They traveled in mid-sized ships that were large enough to sail in the open sea but small enough to navigate through the rivers of Europe. The Vikings were expert warriors and were known to steal and torture their victims. With fearsome names, like "Eric the Blood Axe", the Vikings were feared throughout Western Europe and no one was safe from their attacks.

Which areas did the Vikings conquer?

The Vikings did not stop at attacking and raiding Western Europe; they also established colonies throughout the world. They settled in Greenland, Iceland, parts of France and Great Britain, North America, Ukraine, and Russia.

Why were castles so important in the middle ages?

Castles were built by European nobilities as places of shelter fortified to protect them from attacks during raids by Vikings and other tribes of the middle ages. The main defences of castles were their thick walls, secret passages, moats, drawbridges and defenders. The defenders were usually archers who fired arrows through slits in the castle walls. Though the castles protected the nobles, there were some disadvantages too – they were usually cold, isolated and lacking in hygiene.

When did feudalism start in Europe?

Because of the constant attack by the Vikings and other nomad tribes, the governments of Europe struggled and this led to shambled economies and disrupted trade. When the current type of government lost power a new type of government evolved called Feudalism. Feudalism began in France around 900 A.D. and spread throughout the rest of Europe in 150 years.

Who were the Lords and Knights of medieval Europe?

Feudalism started when the monarchs started giving local territories for their lords to control. These lords controlled all aspects of life within their territories. Along with the lands they were given they also owned the peasants who lived on their land. In exchange for this full control on their territories, the lords pledged their loyalty to the king and promised to supply him with knights for his armies. Often a lord would have lesser lords who he controlled and greater lords who he was loyal to.

What do you mean by Knighthood?

Becoming a knight was a very important for Lords during medieval times. Sons of lords started training for knighthood at the age of 7. By 15, they became squires. A squire was assigned as an apprentice to a knight and he followed the knight and assisted him in his duties. When a squire successfully proved his worth and strength in battle, he would then be knighted in an elaborate ceremony.

What was the inquisition?

In the year 1232 A.D. the Catholic Church established a court known as the Inquisition. The Inquisition was given the responsibility of seeking out and punishing heretics (a person who had religious beliefs that were different from that of the church). Often individuals were charged with heresy with little or no proof. The courts would torture these individuals in order to get a confession from them. If these individuals confessed and repented, they would be forgiven. If not, they would be punished, with punishments including imprisonment, loss of titles and death.

What is Chivalry?

Knights were guided by a certain code of conduct or ethics called chivalry. Chivalry promoted honesty, fairness in battle and proper treatment of noble women. This code of conduct associated with chivalry gradually blended with the expectations of proper manners for a gentleman in todays western culture.

Who were the crusaders?

The city of Jerusalem was the center of faith for three major world religions and for the Jews, it was their homeland. In 600 A.D. the holy land of the Jews was conquered by Islam and would remain in its control for many centuries to come. In 1095 A.D. Pope Urban II called for volunteers to travel to Jerusalem and fight

the Muslims and take back Jerusalem from them. He called their mission a 'crusade'. The word 'crusade' comes from the word crux meaning 'cross' in Latin. Those who volunteered for the crusade were called crusaders.

What was the Hundred Years' War?

The Hundred Years' War was a number of conflicts that erupted between England and France and is generally considered to have lasted 116 years, beginning in 1337 and ending in 1453.

Why was the 'War of Roses' so called?

The 'War of Roses' was fought between 1455 and 1485 by the house of Lancaster, which bore emblem of a 'red rose' and the Duke of York, whose family bore the emblem of a 'white rose'. For a total of 30 years the house of Lancaster and the house of York were at war for the control of England. In the end, the Duke of York was successful finally ending the long-fought civil war.

THE RENAISSANCE AND THE REFORMATION

What was the Renaissance?

During the middle ages, people lived in poor conditions for hundreds of years - a period referred to as the 'Dark ages' in history. But something happened in mid 1300's that changed things – it was Renaissance. 'Renaissance' is french for 'Rebirth'. It was a glorious period when people began thinking of new ideas and developments in art, beauty, architecture, science, literature, mathematics, technology and many other fields. The idea was to rediscover art and science the way ancient Greeks and Romans did!

What did the Renaissance contribute to the world?

Some of the greatest contributions of the Renaissance period are beautiful works of art, sculptures and literature. New musical instruments were invented and existing ones were enhanced. The printing press was invented by Gutenberg and greatly helped spread knowledge. In the field of science there were great advancements in anatomy and scientists started studying about the universe in detail.

When did the Renaissance begin?

The Renaissance began around 1350 A.D. in Italy and continued till about 1600 A.D. Historians believe that the creativity and imagination of thinkers, artists and scientists in the renaissance led to the beginning of a modern era.

Who were some famous personalities of the Renaissance?

Some famous people of the Renaissance include: Leonardo da Vinci, Michelangelo, Shakespeare, Medici, Galileo, Copernicus, Columbus, Marco Polo and Gutenberg. Their contributions to the society came in the form of art, sculptures, literature, scientific discoveries, world exploration and inventions.

What were some of the contributions of Leonardo da Vinci?

Leonardo da Vinci was a polymath – he excelled in a lot of things! He was a master artist, sculptor, scientist, engineer and anatomist. Thanks to his habit of recording all his research in detail, we know about flying machines, anatomical studies, nature and other subjects that he had studied! He developed ideas for bicycles, parachutes, helicopters and even airplanes about 500 years before they were designed!

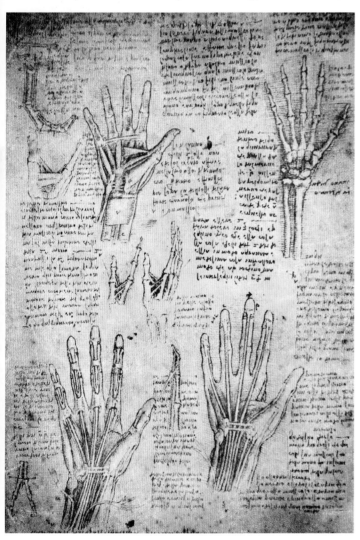

What was the Reformation?

As the Renaissance spread throughout Europe, the standard of living among Europeans greatly improved – and so did knowledge! Many educated people who read the Bible realized that the Catholic Church was spending extravagantly and abusing people – all in the name of God. They thought that the Church practices were not consistent with the teachings found in the scriptures. This resulted in the 'Protestant Reformation.'

Who was Martin Luther?

The protestant reformation began with the efforts of a German monk whose name was Martin Luther. Greatly upset by the corruption he observed in many Roman monasteries, he decided to dedicate his life to learning and teaching the Gospel. He translated the Bible in the German language, to encourage people to read it in their own language and understand its true meaning.

Who was John Calvin?

In the middle of the 15th century, another religious leader by the name of John Calvin began working towards bringing a reformation in the Catholic Church. Calvin lived in Switzerland, and wanted to setup a theocracy or church rule. By the year 1541, John Calvin succeeded in setting up his theocracy in Geneva. This government forced all its citizens to attend church several times a week and had very strict rules about what people could or could not do!

MEDIEVAL ASIA

What was Asia like in the middle Ages?

Researchers believe that during the middle Ages, Asia had made enormous advancements in the field of warfare, science and communication. Paper, porcelain, silk and the mariner's compass are just a few of inventions that were unique to Asia in the middle ages! To get an idea, gunpowder was available in Asia as far back as in the 11th century while it appeared in Europe only in the mid 13th century. A moveable type of printing press was widely used, about 500 years before Gutenberg invented the printing press.

Who were the Mongols?

In the northern part of central Asia, a group of nomads isolated from the rest of the world thrived. These nomads were called the Mongols and their name is derived from their homeland, which was known as Mongolia. Because of this isolation, they were protected from outsiders, thus allowing them to grow from strength to strength. Like all nomads, they migrated from place to place and lived in tents and harsh climate encouraged them to be fierce and ruthless in order to survive!

Who was Genghis Khan?

In the 12th century, a tribal leader who emerged in Mongolia changed the fate of the people of Asia for centuries – he was Genghis Khan! His name was originally Temujin and his father was a minor Mongol chieftain. In 1206, Temujin organized a council and proclaimed himself as the leader of Mongols. He united the different Mongol tribes and set laws called "yasa" that all citizens had to follow! He also established and made sure that they had the best weaponry and training of any army on Earth at the time. His power and successes earned him the title 'Genghis Khan'.

What do we know about Vietnam in the middle ages?

Vietnam was under Chinese rule from 200 B.C. to 939 A.D. Because of this, the culture that survives in Vietnam resembles the culture in China. However that does not mean Vietnam completely lost their own culture. They did manage to retain many aspects of their own culture, language, religious beliefs and customs – one of which includes body tattooing! The Vietnamese under the leadership of their hero, a general by the name of Ngo Quyen, defeated a fleet of Chinese warships, which led to the eventual end of Chinese rule in Vietnam.

Who are the people of Thailand descendants of?

The people of modern day Thailand are descendants of a group of people known as the Thai. The word 'Thai' means 'free men'. Originally from China, they began migrating south in around 700 A.D. and by the 12th century, they were able to establish a successful and thriving civilization with Sukhothai as its capital. After Sukhothai, Ayutthaya was the capital of Thailand for about 400 years. Sukhothai and Ayutthaya are today UNESCO world heritage sites!

What is Sumo wrestling?

Believe it or not, Sumo wrestling started off as a ritual to the gods to pray for a good harvest! Sumo matches, dances and dramas were organized as a part of this ritual in shrines. Sumo wrestling became a popular spectator sport under the patronage of kings and royal families between 710 and 1185 AD. These wrestlers were treated with much respect in the middle ages and enjoyed free meals and celebrity status!

Who were the Samurai?

The samurai, also called bushi, were Japanese warriors of military class who emerged in the 8th century! They used a range of weapons such as bows and arrows, spears and guns, but the weapon that they were most famous for was the sword! The warriors were supposed to live according to a warrior code called 'bushido'. Some of the most common qualities that defined samurai are high sense of duty, loyalty and obedience and honour.

HOW A BABY FORMS

How is a baby made?

The formation of a baby is a remarkable process. It begins when the sperm from a man's body travels into a woman's body. Here in the woman's body, the sperm travels through the fallopian tube and fuses with the egg that is present there. After a few days, the fused egg moves through the fallopian tube and lands into the uterus where it starts growing into a fetus.

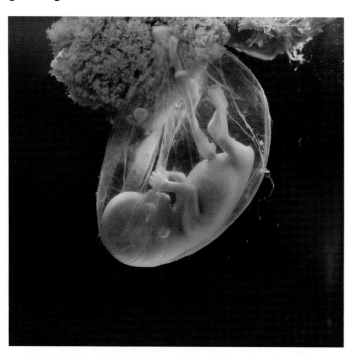

When does a baby start developing?

When a sperm fuses with the egg in a woman's body, the fertilized egg moves to the uterus where it becomes a foetus and placenta. The placenta acts as a life support system for the fetus and delivers oxygen, nutrients and hormones from the mother to the fetus during the entire pregnancy.

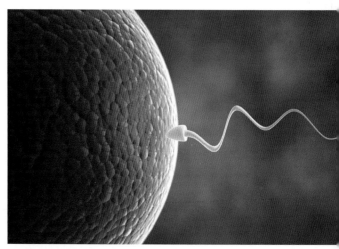

What is the umbilical cord?

Inside a mother's body, the baby gets nutrients from what the mother eats or drinks and oxygen from what she breathes through the umbilical cord. Any waste that is generated by the baby is also expelled out through this cord! The umbilical cord is a flexible tube that connects from placenta to the developing baby's navel or tummy button.

weeks

| 1 | 2 | 3 | 4 | 5 | 6 | 7 | 8 | 9 | 16 | 20-36 | 38 |

How long does a pregnancy last?

A normal pregnancy lasts for 280 days (about 40 weeks), counting from the first day of the last menstrual period. A normal range, however, is from as few as 259 days to as many as 294 days. The 40 weeks of pregnancy are divided into three trimesters. These last about 12–13 weeks each (or about 3 months)

What happens in the first trimester?

The first 12 weeks of pregnancy is considered to make up the first trimester. During this period, fertilization happens and the woman goes through many physical changes due to a temporary increase in hormones. She is also likely to experience 'morning sickness' where she might feel nausea that could lead to vomiting and lethargy.

What happens in the second trimester?

The woman enters into the second trimester when she is in her 13th week of pregnancy and which usually lasts until her 28th week. During this period most women feel more energized and begin to put on weight as the symptoms of morning sickness subside and eventually fade away. In the 20th week, the uterus can expand to up to 20 times its normal size!

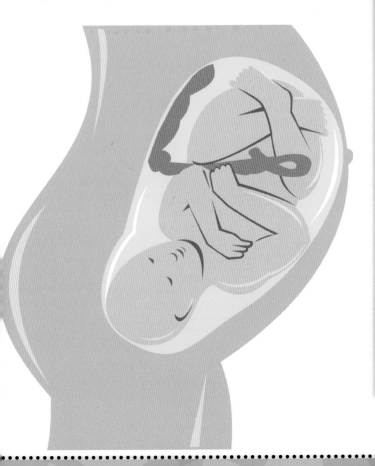

What happens in the third trimester?

At this stage the baby is fully formed and it can open and close its eyes and use all its five senses. The baby's heart pumps around 300 gallons of blood per day! About one week before the birth, the woman's belly will transform in shape as the belly drops due to the baby moving into a downward position ready for birth.

What is the due date and why is it important?

Calculating the due date or the "estimated date of delivery" or EDD is very important because it is used as a guide to check the baby's growth and also to gauge how the pregnancy progresses. The EDD gives a rough idea of when the baby will be born.

Daily Countdown to Due Date	Daily Count forward to Due Date	Pregnancy Week	Weeks after Conception	Pregnancy Month	Lunar Month	Trimester
280-274	1-7	0	Period			
273-267	8-14	1		1st Month (Month 0)	Month One	
266-260	15-21	2	Ovulation			
259-253	22-28	3	Conception			
252-246	29-35	4	1		Month Two	
245-238	36-42	5	2	2nd Month (Month 1)		First Trimester
237-232	43-49	6	3			
231-225	50-56	7	4			
224-218	57-63	8	5		Month Three	
217-211	64-70	9	6			
210-204	71-77	10	7	3rd Month (Month 2)		
203-197	78-84	11	8			
196-190	85-91	12	9			
189-183	92-98	13	10		Month Four	
182-176	99-105	14	11	4th Month (Month 3)		
175-169	106-112	15	12			
168-162	113-119	16	13			
161-155	120-126	17	14		Month Five	
154-148	127-133	18	15	5th Month (Month 4)		Second Trimester
147-141	134-140	19	16			
140-134	141-147	20	17			
133-127	148-154	21	18		Month Six	
126-120	155-161	22	19	6th Month (Month 5)		
119-113	162-168	23	20			

OUR LIFE CYCLE

What are the different stages in life?

Like animals and plants, humans also go through a life cycle. This includes a number of stages starting from birth to death. They include stages of fertilization, infancy, childhood, adolescence, adulthood, old age and eventually death.

When does the human life cycle start?

Studies have pointed out that humans go through a life cycle with life beginning during the fertilization of the egg to form a fetus, which then grows inside the mother and after a period of about 9 months results in a baby being born. At this stage in life the baby is called an infant.

What is the infancy stage?

When a fetus is delivered it is called an infant. It is considered to be the start of its life, although life does start before that, this is the point in life that the baby can physically survive without its mother. For the first year of an infant's life, the infant entirely depends upon its parents to provide shelter, protection and food.

When does a human grow the most and the fastest after birth?

During the first year after birth, infants grow rapidly. Most infants triple their birth weight, grow teeth, start talking and learn to walk in the first year after their birth.

When does an infant become a child?

When an infant is over a year old it is considered a child. This is another period of rapid growth, but the growth rate is not nearly as fast as that of the infant stage of the human life cycle. During this time the child learns to communicate with people using language, solve problems and perform tasks. The childhood stage lasts for approximately 10 to 12 years.

When does a child become an adolescent?

Humans enter adolescence between the ages of 11 and 13. At this time, the body undergoes rapid changes as it prepares itself for reproduction and adulthood.

What are the changes that can be seen in the human body during adolescence?

Sexual organs develop and the differences between male and female sexes become more obvious. Men are larger with more muscle mass, while women have twice the body fat of men. Most female humans reach maturity and stop growing in their late teens or early 20's. This happens to most human males in their early or in their mid-20's.

How many years does adulthood last?

This is perhaps the longest stage in the human life cycle. It is common for adulthood to last 50 years or more. At this stage most people reproduce and raise their own children.

When do humans stop reproducing?

When humans are in their 50's most women lose the ability to reproduce and most men experience a noticeable drop in testosterone levels.

When does the human life cycle end?

The human life cycle ends when there is no more brain activity. It is usually caused by organ failure when the brain can no longer be nourished by the body, which typically happens in the 80's or 90's. Disease or trauma can cause premature death in humans at any time.

BONES IN OUR BODY

What would happen if humans didn't have bones?

Imagine a human body without bones. Could you stand up? Forget it! Could you walk? No way! Without bones the body would not be able to move. Bones form part of what is known as the skeletal system of our body.

What are the two purposes that bones serve?

Bones serve a very important purpose because without the skeletal system there would be no structure to our body. Our skeletal system is what keeps our body in shape. Another important purpose that the skeletal system provides is that it protects our vital organs, such as the heart, brain, and lungs.

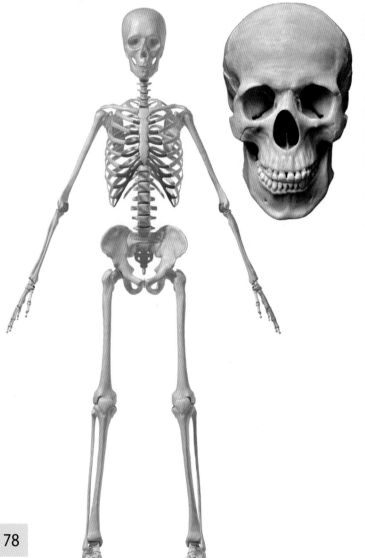

How many bones do we have?

When a baby is born, it has 300 bones. However when it grows up some of the bones begin to fuse together resulting in an adult human having only 206 bones.

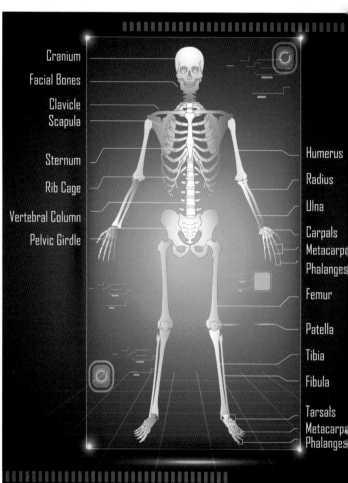

Cranium
Facial Bones
Clavicle
Scapula
Sternum
Rib Cage
Vertebral Column
Pelvic Girdle
Humerus
Radius
Ulna
Carpals
Metacarpals
Phalanges
Femur
Patella
Tibia
Fibula
Tarsals
Metacarpals
Phalanges

How do my bones move?

Bones are very important because along with muscles and joints, they help the body to move. When the muscles contract, the bones that are attached to them act as levers making the other body parts move.

What are joints?

Joints in the human body are very important because they form a flexible connection between the bones. The body has different kinds of joints. Joints in the knees work like door hinges, hence we can move back and forth, while the joints on the head and neck enable us to nod, turn and tilt our head. The ball joints on the arms and legs enable us to move them 360 degrees.

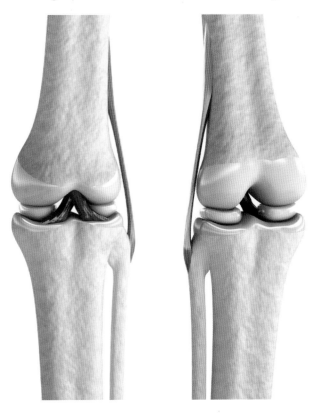

Are bones alive?

Yes, in the body, bones do have life in them. They are made of a mix of hard matter than gives them strength and many living cells in the marrow that help them grow and repair on their own. Like all the cells in our body, the bones depend on blood to keep them functional.

What is bone marrow?

At the center of most of the bones there is thick jelly, called marrow, that makes red and white blood cells. The red blood cells ensure that oxygen is distributed to all parts of the body, while white blood cells fight germs and disease.

What is the longest and smallest bone in the human body?

The longest bone is the thigh bone, the femur which is about 1/4 of your height. The smallest is the stirrup bone in the ear which measures about 1/10th of an inch.

Is there any bone that is not connected to any other bone in the human body?

The hyoid bone, which is the only bone in the throat, is not connected to any other bone in the body! It is connected instead, to ligaments which are strong fibrous tissue that connect bones. The hyoid bone helps in movement of tongue, larynx and pharynx by connecting the muscles in this region.

MUSCLE EFFECT

Why are muscles important to us?

Muscles are just as important as bones for providing any kind of movement in the body – be it lifting a heavy backpack, shrugging your shoulder or even raising your eyebrows. Without muscles we will not be able to stand, walk, run or sit! Muscles make up nearly half of the weight of the human body.

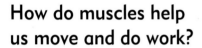

How do muscles help us move and do work?

Muscles provide force so that the body can move. Muscles are made of many fibres and stretch across joints to link one bone with another and work in groups to respond to the impulse sent out by the nerves.

What are the different types of muscles?

There are three major types of muscles in the body: skeletal, smooth, and cardiac.

What are skeletal muscles?

As their name implies, skeletal muscles are attached to the skeleton and help move various parts of the body. These muscles are made up of tissue fibres that are striated or striped. They are also called voluntary muscles because you control their use, such as flexing of an arm or raising the foot. There are over 650 skeletal muscles in the whole human body!

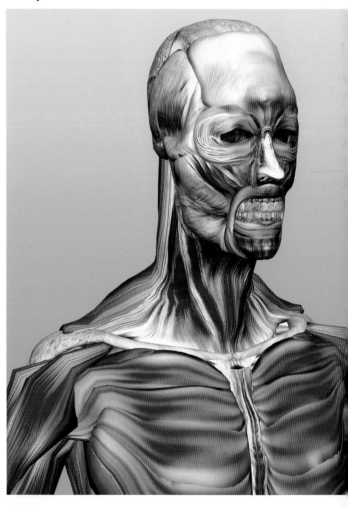

Where are smooth muscles generally found?

Smooth muscles are found in our internal organs like in our digestive system and blood vessels. They are called involuntary muscles because a person generally cannot consciously control them. Their movement is controlled by the autonomic nervous system. Unlike the skeletal muscles, smooth muscles have no striations or stripes.

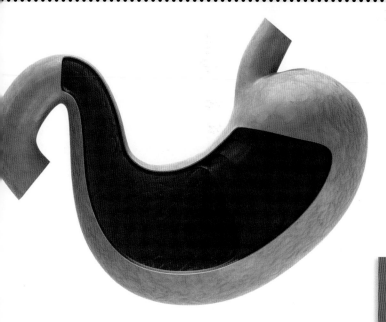

difficulty in swallowing. Vaccinations are administered for preventing tetanus too. Muscular dystrophy is a disease that is caused when the genes that code for a protein, that helps to keep muscles healthy and fit, is missing. The person with this disease slowly loses the ability to do simple things like sitting or walking.

Is the tongue the strongest muscle in the body?

The tongue is made up of a group of muscles that help in mixing up food, speaking, pushing saliva down the throat and filtering germs. While it is popularly quoted that the tongue is the strongest muscle in the human body, scientists believe that the credit actually goes to the jaw muscle. And in terms of endurance and non-stop working, the heart muscle takes the prize!

What type of muscle is the heart made of?

Also called the myocardium, the cardiac muscle is only found in the heart! It is a very unique type of muscle that is composed of thick twisted ring like arrangements. This muscle forms the walls of the chambers of the heart. When it contracts, blood is pumped throughout the body.

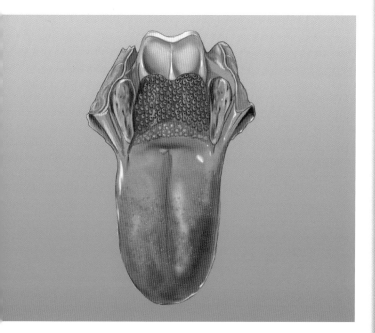

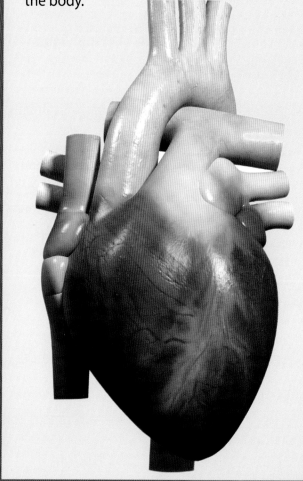

What are some diseases that affect muscles?

Polio is a virus infection that causes paralysis of muscles. Thanks to polio vaccinations, the disease occurs much less frequently than before. Tetanus also called 'Lock jaw' causes spasms of facial muscles and

FOOD FOR THE BODY

How does food travel in the body?

It is easy to forget what happens to the food once we eat it - however it is quite an interesting process! After the food that we eat reaches our stomachs, it has to be broken down into even smaller pieces before it can travel through the rest of our body. The process is complex and requires some important enzymes in our digestive system to break down the food particles.

What are all the organs that make up the digestive tract?

The various organs that make up the digestive tract are the mouth, esophagus, stomach, small intestine, large intestine (colon) rectum, and anus.

How does the food we eat get all mashed up?

After you chew your food with your teeth and break it into manageable pieces, the saliva gets into action! It helps to break down food and form a small ball of food ready to swallow. This is called the bolus. The digestive system receives the bolus and breaks it down even further to provide nutrients to build and nourish cells and provide energy.

What happens to the food in the esophagus?

The esophagus is a pipe-like structure that is about 10 inches long. The bolus is pushed through the throat when a flap called the epiglottis opens up and this flap makes sure that the food enters the esophagus and not the windpipe by mistake! After entering the esophagus the food does not just drop into the stomach. Instead, the muscles in the esophagus gently moves the food in a wave-like manner into the stomach.

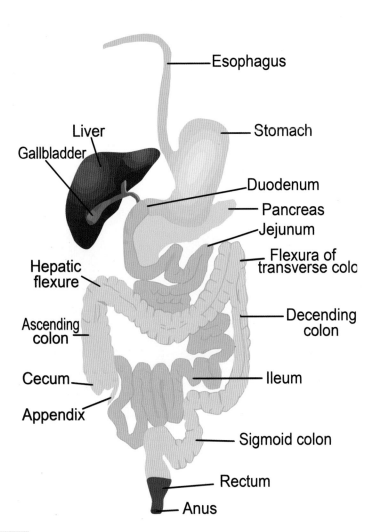

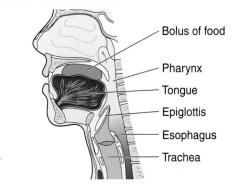

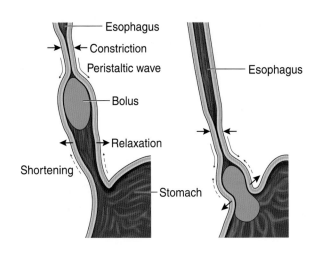

What causes heartburn?

The esophagus has a ring of muscles on both ends. If the muscles at the bottom do not keep esophagus tightly closed between swallows, stomach acids might come back into the esophagus! This causes a burning sensation or pain and is called heartburn. It has nothing to do with the heart though!

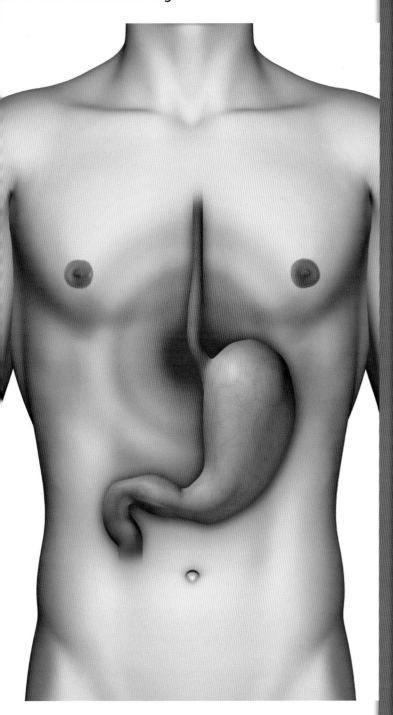

Why is digestion important?

When we eat food such as bread, meat or vegetables, they are not in a form that the body can readily use as nourishment. Whatever we eat or drink must be changed into smaller molecules of nutrients before they can be absorbed into the blood and carried to cells throughout the body.

What are the two most important organs of the digestive system?

Although all the organs of the digestive system are important to help digest food, there are two important digestive organs, the liver and the pancreas. Both these organs produce digestive juices that reach the intestine through small tubes called ducts. The gallbladder stores the liver's digestive juices until they are needed in the intestine.

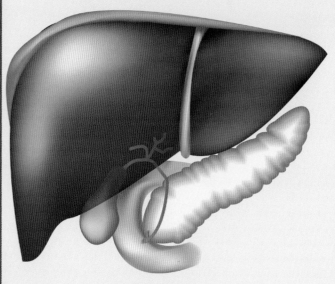

What does the large intestine do?

After most of the nutrients in the food have been used, the leftover digested food passes through the colon region of the large intestine. This is the last place for any remaining nutrients and water in the digested food to be absorbed! After passing through the large intestine, it is expelled as solid waste or faeces.

Why is the heart important to the human body?

The heart is one of the most important organs in the human body. Without it a human being cannot function. The heart is a hard-working organ that functions as a pump. It is composed of strong muscles that constantly flex and pump blood throughout the body!

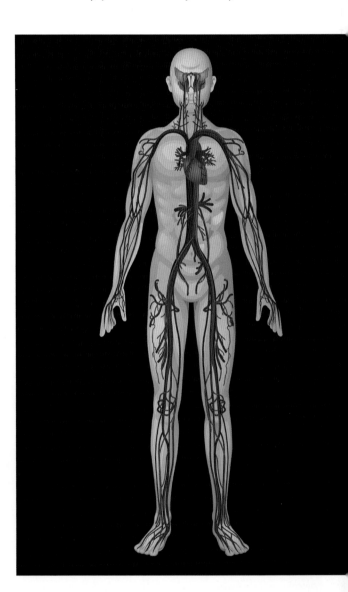

Why does the heart need to pump blood throughout the body?

The heart needs to pump blood because the blood carries all the vital materials which help our bodies function and also removes the waste products that we do not need. Take the brain or muscles for instance - these need oxygen and glucose. If they do not receive them continuously, a person can lose consciousness or die. If the heart ever ceases

to pump blood the body begins to shut down and after a very short while the person would die.

How does the heart function?

With each heartbeat, blood is sent around our bodies, carrying oxygen and nutrients to every cell. Each day 2000 gallons of blood travels through the equivalent length of 60,000 miles of blood vessels that branch and link the cells, organs and other various body parts. What a journey!

How does the heart manage to send blood to all parts of the body?

Thanks to the blood vessels, which along with the heart form the circulatory system, blood is transported from head to toe! These blood vessels include arteries, veins and capillaries. The heart not only supplies fresh blood to every part of the body, it also collects used-up blood and pumps it to the lungs for re-oxygenating!

What does the heart consist of?

The heart has four chambers that are enclosed by thick, muscular walls. The bottom part of the heart is divided into two chambers called the right and left ventricles that pump blood out of the heart, while the upper part of the heart is made up of the other two chambers of the heart, the right and left atria. All these 4 hear chambers work together as a team to pump blood across the body and keep us fit!

How do arteries help in circulation?

Arteries are the thickest blood vessels that carry blood away from the heart. They contract to keep the blood moving away from the heart and through the body. As they get farther from the heart, the arteries branch out into tinier tubes called arterioles.

What are veins?

Veins carry blood from the body back to the heart. Unlike arteries, they are not muscular. They contain valves that prevent blood from flowing backward.

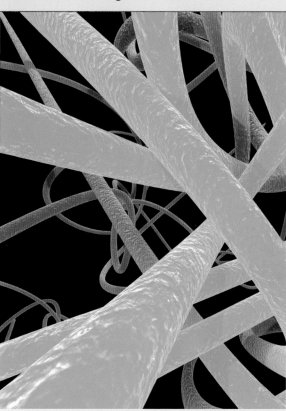

What connects the veins to the arteries?

A capillary is an extremely small blood vessel that transports blood from arteries to veins.

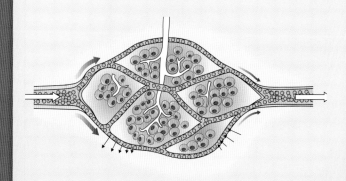

THE 5 SENSES

What senses are in the human body?

Whenever we hear phrases like what's that smell? Do you hear that? Taste this! Look at me! Feel this, isn't it too soft? We generally do not stop to think about them. As humans we can do all of these things because certain organs in our body, known as the sense organs, take in information they get from contact with an object or our surrounding and send it to the brain for processing. If we didn't have them we would not be able to smell, see, hear, taste or touch anything.

How many sense organs do we have?

We have five main sense organs. They are the eyes, nose, ears, tongue, and skin. Some scientists however are of the opinion that we actually have nine senses: sight, sound, taste, touch, smell, pain, balance, thirst and hunger.

How do our eyes help us see?

Sight is probably the most developed sense in humans. Our eyes help to focus and detect visible light through photoreceptors in the retina of each eye. These generate electrical nerve impulses for varying colours, hues and brightnesses. There are two types of photoreceptors: rods and cones. Rods help in day vision while cones help us see at night.

The eye must do the following things to help us see:

- An image must be reduced to fit onto the retina

- The light from the object must be focused on the retina surface

- The information about the image should be quickly sent to the brain to be processed!

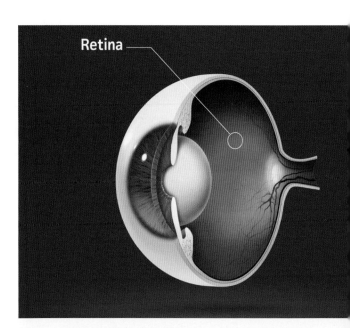

Retina

Why do some people wear glasses?

It is common to see people wearing glasses to help them to see better! Two common eye complaints are called Myopia and Hyperopia. Myopia occurs when distant objects look blurred because the images come into focus before the retina. Hyperopia occurs when near objects do not come into focus before the retina. Both of these can be corrected by wearing specially designed eye glasses.

How can some animals like dogs hear sounds we don't hear?

Sounds come in different frequency ranges. We humans can hear only sounds that have pitches ranging between 20 hertz and 20,000 hertz. Any sound above or below this frequency range cannot be heard by us. But animals like dogs and mice can detect sounds above this frequency range. Take the dog whistle for instance – it produces a single note of high pitch that can be heard only by dogs, because they have a hearing range greater than ours!

How do we hear sounds?

The outer ear sticks out away from the head and collects and directs sounds toward the tympanic membrane. The vibrations are directed to the inner ear through a series of small bones in the middle ear. The inner ear is a spiral-shaped chamber that reacts to the vibrations and then transmits impulses to the brain through the auditory nerve. The brain combines the input of the two ears to determine the direction and distance of the sound.

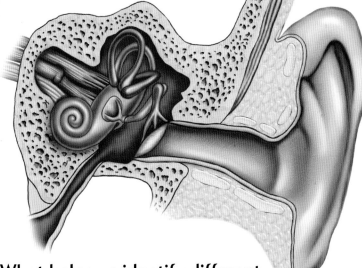

What helps us identify different taste types?

The sense of taste is important because without it we would not be able to enjoy food the way we do. There are 'taste buds' or receptors on the tongue that detect different tastes. The taste buds on top and on the side of the tongue are sensitive to salty and sour tastes whereas those in the back of the tongue are sensitive to bitter tastes.

How are tastes affected when the nose is blocked?

When you have a cold or when you hold your nose tight when you taste food, it doesn't quite have the right flavour. Why? Because the olfactory receptors in the nose help us taste too! These receptors work together with the taste buds to help you identify the true taste of food. Next time, thank both your tongue and your nose after you eat a yummy dessert!

How does the nose help us smell different things?

The nose, unlike the taste buds, has hundreds of olfactory receptors. These special receptors have a variety of features and one of them is to stimulate certain receptors more or less strongly. This combination of stimulation signals from different receptors makes up what we perceive as the molecule's smell. Olfactory receptor neurons in the nose differ from most other neurons because they die and regenerate on a regular basis.

How does the sense of touch work?

The sense of touch is the only one of the senses that is found all over the body! This is because the sense of touch originates in the bottom layer of the skin called the dermis. The dermis is filled with many small nerve endings which give the brain information about the things the body comes in contact with. The information is carried along the spinal cord to the brain where the feeling is registered.

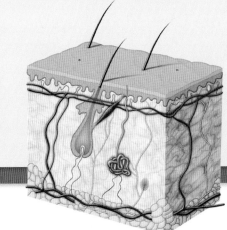

What is light made of?

Light is made of millions and millions of tiny particles called photons! The photons travel from one place to another in the form of waves. Of all the different photons that are in visible light, the ones that have the longest wavelength appear red to us, and the ones that have the shortest wavelength look blue. All the colours come from different wavelengths of light.

Where does the Earth get light from?

The Earth gets its light from the Sun. The Sun shoots out billions of photons every second in all directions and the ones that are pointed toward the Earth come here. When these photons get to the Earth, they pass through the Earth's atmosphere.

What are Ultra Violet Rays?

Ultraviolet or UV rays are invisible rays that are part of the light energy that comes from the sun. UV rays can be very harmful to the human body – it can burn the eyes, hair and skin if people are over exposed to it. But the good thing is most of the ultraviolet rays have a short wavelength and are absorbed in the atmosphere. Otherwise UV rays would kill almost all living things on Earth!

What are infrared rays?

Infrared or IR rays are light rays with wavelengths that are longer than visible light, but shorter than microwave radiation. The heat we feel from the sun, a hot oven or a fire are all infrared rays! Infrared rays are often used in television remote controls because they do not interfere with the television signal itself. Some fast food restaurants use special infrared lamps to heat the food so that we can enjoy piping hot dishes!

Does light move at the same speed everywhere?

No! Light moves at the rate of about 300,000,000 metres per second only in a vacuum. But it slows down considerably when it moves through substances like atmosphere, water or glass. Do you know that light travels at the rate of 124,000,000 metres per second when it is passing through a diamond? That is about half its usual speed!

How do gas lamps work?

Fluorescent lamps, sodium vapour lamps, neon signs – these all are examples of gas discharge lamps. When an electric current is passed through certain gases, they emit light. These gas lamps come in different colours which vary depending on the type of gas used and the way the lamp is constructed.

What are lenses and what do we do with them?

Lenses are curved pieces of transparent glass that bend light rays which pass through them and cause light to change direction! Convex lens make light rays bend and meet at a spot called the focal point. They are used in binoculars and telescopes to bring light rays from distance to focus in your eyes so that you'll be able to see them better. Concave lens help spread the light rays outward. These are used in TV projectors and flashlights.

How can a magnifying glass start a fire?

On a sunny day, a magnifying glass can be used to start a fire if you are out camping and forgot to bring a box of matches! How does it work? The convex lens in the magnifying glass concentrates sunlight on a small area causing the intense beams of sunlight to start a fire. For the same reason it is dangerous to look at the sun using a magnifying glass, binoculars, telescope or even the naked eye!

How do lasers work?

What makes a laser different from ordinary light is that in a laser, more and more energy is added to light so that it becomes extremely concentrated. It means that all the light waves in a laser have the same wavelength and move completely in step. A machine is used to pump billions of photons all at once so that they line up to form a very concentrated beam! No wonder lasers can bore holes through paper, cloth, plastics, ceramics and even metals!

How are shadows formed?

Shadows are formed when a particular solid object blocks out light rays – as a result the shadow takes the shape of the object! The object has to be opaque or at least translucent to form a shadow. In other words, a shadow is an absence of light in a particular area.

ELECTRICITY

What exactly is electricity?

In order to understand electricity, it is necessary to explore atoms closely. Atoms are made up of protons and neutrons in the nucleus and electrons revolving around it. Electrons can move from atom to atom and this movement of electrons causes a charge to move which we measure as a current.

What is charge?

Some atoms have loosely attached electrons and these atoms lend or accept electrons easily. An atom that loses or gains electrons is considered to be charged. Atoms that have more electrons than protons are negatively charged and those that have fewer electrons than protons are positively charged. Charged atoms are called 'ions'.

Can electric charge pass through all materials?

Electricity or electric current passes through some materials better than the others. Materials like glass, wood, cloth and plastic hold on to electrons very tightly and do not let them pass freely. Hence these materials are poor conductors of electricity and called 'insulators'. Metals conduct electricity well because the electrons are held loosely and these are called 'conductors'. Electric wires are usually made of metals like copper that conduct electricity well.

Why is it dangerous to touch a switch with a wet hand?

Water and our body are also good conductors of electricity! Electricity from a switch travels through water on a wet hand and gives an electric shock. It is dangerous to touch any electrical appliances without proper protection or wet hands!

What is the most natural form of electricity?

Electricity in its most natural form is seen during a thunderstorm when lightning bolts strike down from the sky and you can see the power that electricity has. A bolt of lightning is a sudden, massive surge of electricity between the sky and the ground beneath. Did you know that a single lightning bolt is enough to light 100 powerful lamps for a whole day or to make a couple of hundred thousand slices of toast!

How did Benjamin Franklin prove that lightning conducts electricity?

In the 18th century, Benjamin Franklin conducted a simple experiment to prove that lightning is an electrical discharge. One stormy day he flew a kite with a key attached to it. When the kite touched upon the storm clouds an electric charge passed through the kite string to the key. When Franklin touched the key, he observed sparks and felt a shock. It was a dangerous experiment but it helped him invent the lightning rod that protects buildings from lightning.

How do batteries make electricity?

Battery stores chemical energy which can produce electricity when it is connected to a circuit. You must have noticed batteries having a positive and negative terminal. Connecting a wire between these two terminals causes a chemical reaction to take place inside the battery. This reaction in turn generates 'ions' that conduct electricity for lighting up your flashlight or making your toy work.

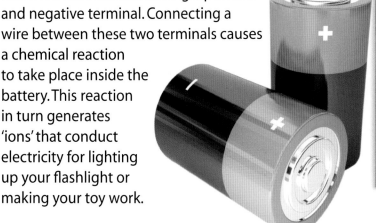

Where does electricity we use come from?

In today's world, power plants are responsible for producing electricity out of other forms of energy. Most of the electricity in the world today comes from converting the heat energy released from burning fossil fuels like coal, natural gas and oil. The rest is generated from nuclear reactors and from renewable sources such as sunlight, wind, water etc.

What does the word electricity mean?

The word electricity comes from the Greek word 'elektron' which means 'amber'. Amber is a hardened plant resin and ancient Greeks found that when amber was rubbed against fur it attracted feathers. This is a classic example of static electricity – a phenomenon unknown at that time!

What is static electricity?

Static electricity is the result of an imbalance between positive and negative charge on objects. When you rub a balloon on a sweater and take it away, it tries to go back and stick to the sweater. The reason? Some electrons are transferred from the sweater to the balloon. The sweater is now positively charged after giving away electrons and the balloon is negatively charged after acquiring electrons. Since they have opposite charges, they attract each other.

WRITING AND PRINTING

How did people express ideas before they invented writing?

For several thousand years, pictures were the only form of communication. In the Paleolithic era, about 30-40,000 years ago, people drew and painted on rocks and walls of caves. It is also from about the same period that the oldest fragments of bones and pebbles with notches and marks have been found!

When did people start writing?

During pre historic times, in order to show something or tell a story, people would draw on cave walls or any other suitable surface. As early as 3100 BC, in order to keep track of grain, sheep and other goods, Sumerians used numbers and symbols. Slowly different forms of alphabets, numbers and symbols were developed by civilizations across the world to communicate with each other.

What is cuneiform writing?

Although people had not invented paper yet, they had plenty of clay, so most of the time they wrote on tablets made from clay. They used a sharp river reed like a pen to make the marks. The reeds made triangular marks in the clay and cuneiform writing is a collection of these little triangular marks.

How did the name 'paper' originate?

It is believed that the Egyptians made the earliest kind of paper using papyrus from which paper derives its name. About 5000 years ago, thin strips of papyrus grass were cut, softened with water, pounded thin and dried in the sun to make parchment sheets for writing.

What were Egyptian hieroglyphics?

A form of writing used by the ancient Egyptians included pictures and characters to narrate something and this is known as hieroglyphics. They used more than 2000 hieroglyphic characters in this form of writing which was practiced more than 5000 years ago. The word 'Hieroglyphics' in Greek means 'sacred writing'.

Who invented paper?

Paper is said to have been invented by Tsai Lun, a Chinese court official, in A.D. 105. He experimented with different materials like rags, textile waste and plant fibres. The art of paper-making slowly spread to neighbouring countries but Arabs were responsible for spreading this process to the Middle East, Europe and eventually to the rest of the world.

When was paper mass produced?

When literacy spread, there was an increased need and demand for paper. The production of each sheet by hand could not keep pace with the demand for paper.

This led to the invention of a machine by Louis Nicholas Robert (1761-1828), to produce a continuous reel of paper. Today most paper is made from wood pulp on a Fourdrinier machine and then cut to size.

Who invented the printing press?

Gutenberg invented a printing press in 1450 that created a revolution in the process of publishing books! He designed a mechanical device that was able to produce many copies of text on a page. Before that, books were mainly made in monasteries, where monks painstakingly copied them! The movable metal press could print more than a thousand pages a day. Thanks to Gutenberg, books became readily available to people all over the world.

Which is the earliest known printed book?

The Diamond Sutra is considered to be the earliest surviving printed book to date. Much before Gutenberg invented the printing press, the Chinese used carved wood blocks and ink to transfer text onto papers. This book was printed in the year A.D. 868!

Which were the first newspapers to be printed?

It is said that as early as 59 B.C. handwritten newspapers in Rome called Acta Diurna were circulated among people during the reign of Julius Caesar to keep them informed about important events. Modern printed newspapers first appeared later in Europe. *Relation* was published in Germany in 1605, *Gazette* in France in 1631 and the *London Gazette* was published in England in 1665.

CLOTHES

What did people wear in the ancient times?

Archaeologists believe that the earliest form of clothing might have consisted of fur, leather, leaves or grass that were draped, wrapped or tied around the body. Some archeologists have identified very early sewing needles of bone and ivory from about 30,000 B.C. found near Kostenki, Russia.

Did the Neanderthal people invent clothing?

Scientists believe that the first people known to make clothing were people from the Neanderthal era. At this time the earth's temperature rose and fell dramatically which led to a number of ice ages. The harsh and cold climate demanded clothing to protect their bodies. Neanderthals learned to use the thick, furry hides from animals they killed to keep themselves warm and dry.

What is a kimono?

Kimono is a traditional dress worn by Japanese men and women on special occasions. Historically, the samurai wore kimonos and hakamas which were pants worn over kimonos to protect their legs from scratches while riding on horses!

What are the different materials used for making clothes?

Some of the commonly used materials for making clothes include cotton, wool, leather, fur, silk, nylon, rayon, velvet and polyester. Fashion designers have designed clothes made of unique materials like porcelain pieces and tree bark!

How is silk made and why is it so expensive?

Silk strands are extracted by dropping silk cocoons in boiling water which kills the silkworm. These silk strands are then woven into fabrics. Silkworms feed only on mulberry leaves and it is difficult to grow and culture them. Also, thousands of cocoons are used to make just a yard of silk. Because of this, silk clothing is usually very expensive.

When were jeans invented?

During the California gold rush, strong durable pants were in great demand! Levi Strauss, a young German immigrant, sold pants made of canvas. Later he substituted canvas with a twilled cotton cloth from France. This cloth was called 'Serge de Nimes' and later came to be known as 'denim' and the blue jeans had officially come into existence!

What is bamboo clothing?

The fibres inside the tough bamboo cane can be used for making soft fabrics and clothing. Clothing made of bamboo fibre is soft and does not hold onto body odour like other material – making clothes smell fresh throughout the day. They are also considered to be naturally anti-bacterial and anti-fungal.

How do clothes come in different colours?

Thanks to the dyeing process it is possible to get clothes with the colour and shades of your choice. Dyes are molecules that actually absorb and reflect light at specific wavelengths so that our eyes can see the colours! Natural and synthetic dyes are used in different dyeing processes to produce the final desired colour or pattern on a garment.

Who invented the Mackintoshes?

Charles Mackintosh, a Scottish chemist, invented a method for making waterproof material using rubber dissolved in coal tar naptha. However, this material became stiff in the cold weather and sticky during hot weather. After vulcanized rubber was invented, mackintosh fabrics improved greatly!

What is bulletproof clothing made from?

Most bulletproof clothing and body armours use a tough fibre material called Kevlar. Kevlar is a lightweight fabric almost similar to regular fabrics, but is five times stronger than steel of the same weight! The Kevlar fibres are interlaced together to form a strong dense net. Vectran is another fibre used in bulletproof clothes – it is about 5 to 10 times stronger than steel!

CALCULATIONS

Who invented the zero?

The number '0' is said to have originated in India in the 5th century. It appeared in a book on arithmetic by Indian mathematician, Brahmagupta. It is also believed that zero originated between 400 and 300 B.C. in Babylon. However the zero was used as a placeholder - for instance, to distinguish between 1 and 10.

What symbols are used as ancient Egyptian hieroglyphic numbers?

Ancient Egyptians followed a decimal system that used seven symbols. 1 was shown as a single stroke, 10 as a hobble for cattle, 100 as a coil of rope, 1000 as lotus plant, 10,000 as finger, 100,000 as tadpole or frog and 1,000,000 as the figure of god with arms raised.

What is an abacus?

Abacus is a Latin word which means 'tablet'. The abacus is a calculating device which consists of frames that hold rods with sliding beads. This device was used for making complex calculations not possible using only human fingers or pebbles. Abacus devices have been used for a very long time – as long ago as 500 B.C.!

Who invented fractions?

Fractions were first used as early as 2800 B.C. in the ancient Indus Valley and by Egyptians around 1000 B.C. The Greeks used fractions until the followers of Pythagoras discovered that the square root of two could not be expressed as a fraction. Jain mathematicians in India, in 150 B.C. wrote the "Sthananga Sutra" that contained work on the theory of numbers, arithmetical operations, and operations with fractions!

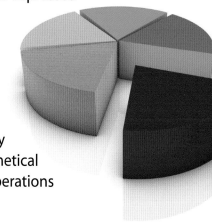

What is the Fibonacci series?

Leonardo Fibonacci, also called Leonardo of Pisa, was an Italian mathematician known for introducing the Arabic numeral system to Europe. He is also known for the famous Fibonacci number series. This series starts with 1 and the next number is the sum of the previous two numbers. So it goes 1, 1, 2, 3, 5, 8, 13, 21 and so on. Interestingly, nature exhibits a Fibonacci series in petals, shell spirals, seeds, leaves and branches, to mention a few!

What was the contribution of Isaac Newton to the field of math?

Isaac Newton was responsible for introducing a new concept in mathematical calculations and it was called 'calculus'. Space engineers, architects, bankers, scientists and many professionals depend on calculus for important calculations.

What is a pie chart?

There are all kinds of charts and graphs. Some of these charts are easy to understand while some of the others can be really troublesome. Pie charts are simple and easy to understand. The entire data is represented as a circle. This circle is divided into sections based on the percentage or value of the data.

What is a matrix?

A matrix is a grid with each space in the grid containing some information. For example, a chess board is a matrix where each and every square contains a specific item of information like a particular chess piece.

Which is the oldest mathematical object known to us?

The Lebombo bone, a piece of bone with 29 clearly marked notches, is said to be about 37,000 years old and considered to be the oldest mathematical object found. It was discovered in a cave between South Africa and Swaziland. It was found to be similar to the calendar sticks used by the bushmen of Africa.

What is an algorithm?

An algorithm is a systematic list of instructions for accomplishing some task. The task can be anything that has an end point. A cooking recipe is one kind of algorithm, for example a recipe for making a potato salad. Steps like "peel the potato" followed by "boil the potato", are instructions and they end when the potato salad is ready to eat.

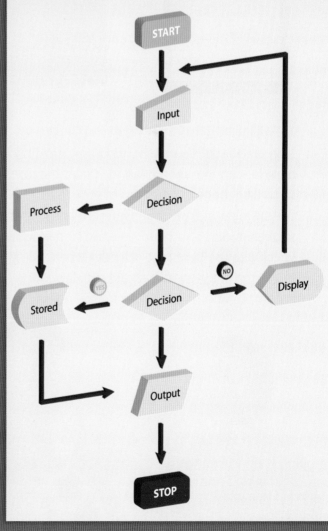

How much has the process of writing changed?

Experts say that written communication has undergone three stages -

- First stage - people used pictures and figures on stone to express their thoughts.

- Then people developed the art of writing and wrote or carved on paper, papyrus, clay, wax etc.

- More recently, information is shared through electronic media and signal technologies.

What is sign language?

Sign language is a system of communicating to people with impaired hearing. It uses gestures, signs and mock expressions of mouth to communicate a message. Different languages are spoken in different countries, and sign languages specific to the language are developed. Many television channels broadcast sign language accompaniments especially for the deaf.

What are radio waves?

Radio waves are invisible electromagnetic waves that can transmit messages, music, pictures and virtually any type of data across millions of miles! Radio waves have different frequencies and a simple radio device requires a transmitter and a receiver to transmit messages using radio signals.

What is a telegraph?

Samuel Morse who invented the Morse code is credited with constructing the electromagnetic telegraph in 1835. A telegraph is a system designed for transmitting information or messages across long distance in the form of signals through electric wires. These signals or pulses are created by making and breaking an electrical connection!

Who invented the television?

Many inventors and scientists have conceptualized and invented various versions of television and it is difficult to give credit to one individual. However, it was John Logie Baird, a Scottish engineer, who first demonstrated in public a working model of a television in 1926.

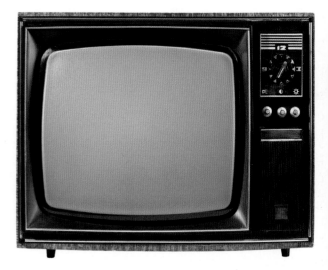

When was the telephone invented?

The telephone is one of the greatest inventions in history. The telephones that first appeared are not the same as the ones we have and use today. In 1876 Alexander Graham Bell invented it when he was trying to invent a device that could send more than one telegram at the same time. Imagine a world without telephones today!

How do pagers work?

Invented by Al Gross in 1949, pagers were widely used until mobile phones replaced them. Also called 'beepers', these portable devices help communicating through messages. A person sent a message by email or touch-tone telephone. This message was forwarded to the pager and the device either beeped or vibrated to alert the owner. The pager then displayed a text message or the originating phone number on a LCD display.

What are walkie-talkies?

Walkie-talkies were invented by the same person who came up with the concept of pagers – Al Gross! These hand-held devices help two or more people communicate with each other through radio wave technology. It has six main parts – transmitter, receiver, channel selector, speaker, microphone and power source. Initially used for military purposes, walkie-talkies soon became available to everyone.

What is the intranet?

An Intranet works on the same principle as the internet – that is, it helps many people access information from available sources. The difference is an intranet is confined to a specific network – for example, school, college, hospital or a particular organization. It allows people only within that network to share information through the local area network, also called LAN.

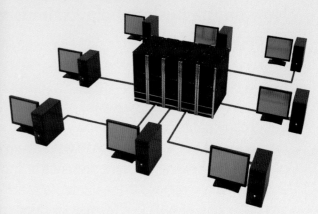

When was the mobile phone invented?

The idea for inventing mobile or cell phones came from mobile car phones as early as 1947. Bell Laboratories were responsible for developing the mobile phone concept. However, it was Martin Cooper of Motorola who invented the first mobile phone in 1973. It is said that he made his first call to Joel Engle, his rival at Bell Laboratories. The first of its kind was available to the public in 1984 – but they were initially heavy and expensive!

TRANSPORT

When were roads constructed?

While it is difficult to pinpoint when roads were first constructed, research has shown that constructed roads must have existed since 3000 B.C. The oldest roads were made of paved stones and timber. Roads these days contain asphalt – the first time asphalt was used in the construction of roads was in 1872 in Pennsylvania, USA.

How do the huskies help Eskimos with transportation?

Huskies are dogs found in the Arctic region that help in pulling sleds. In modern times, snowmobiles have replaced huskies as a means of transportation, but in earlier times people in snowy regions depended on these dog breeds to travel from one place to another. The constant presence of snow and ice in these regions made it impossible to use any other kind of vehicle. A team of six dogs could pull weights of 600 to 700 pounds!

Which is the fastest means of transport?

The aircraft is the fastest method of transport, next only to the rocket. Commercial jets can reach up to 955 kph (593 mph). Aircraft are able to quickly transport people and a limited amount of cargo over longer distances. Researchers are designing supersonic planes for transporting passengers and goods across long distances at faster speeds and with virtually no breaks in flight!

What is the Ornithopter flying machine?

The Ornithopter flying machine does not really exist – it was a model designed by the famous genius, Leonardo da Vinci! The design for this flying machine was sketched out in 1488 and experts believe that the invention of the helicopter was inspired by these drawings!

Who coined the term helicopter?

The term 'helicopter' was coined by the French writer, Ponton D'Amecourt in 1863 and means 'spiral wings'! It was Igor Sikorsky, considered the 'father of helicopters', who came up with the first successful model of helicopter in 1910.

What are maglev trains?

Maglev trains are powered by powerful electromagnets and can achieve very high speeds. Maglev stands for 'magnetic levitation' and a technology called electromagnetic suspension (EMS) helps the train float over a guide way or track made of magnetic coils.

What is a hovercraft?

A hovercraft is an air-cushioned vehicle which is supported by a cushion of air supplied by a fan or engine. This helps the vehicle to lift above the ground or water and it can be steered with specially-designed rudders. It was invented by Christopher Cockerell in 1956.

What is pipeline transport?

With the discovery of oil and associated by-products, pipes were used to transport liquid and gases. Short distance networks are used for transportation of sewage, slurry and water, while long-distance networks are used for petroleum and natural gas.

What are cable cars?

Cable cars are used for transporting people in cabins that are suspended from overhead cables of specific length. These cars can be moved and controlled through the cable by operating a motor and the cars can be stopped by gripping the cable if required.

How do submarines work?

Submarines work on the principle of buoyancy – that is, the submarine vessel can float when the weight of the vessel displaces an equal volume of water. This displacement of water woks in conjunction with the buoyancy and can push the submarine down. To control buoyancy, submarines have ballast tanks or trim tanks that can be filled with air or water. This helps the submarine float or sink at will.

Who invented the first bicycle?

Karl von Drais, a German baron, invented a two-wheeled vehicle propelled by feet in 1817. This pedal-less vehicle was called 'Draisine' and is considered to be the source of inspiration for the modern-day bicycle.

What are some features of Formula One race cars?

Formula One car comprises approximately 80,000 components and can be refueled in a matter of just seconds. While racing car tyres give maximum speed and grip, they are designed to last only for 90 to 120 kilometres. Did you know that most racing car tyres are filled with nitrogen instead of air? This is because nitrogen has more uniform pressure than air over different temperatures.

What is the Tour de France?

The Tour de France is one of the most famous annual bicycle races! This bicycling event was first held in 1903 and it really tests the endurance levels of contestants. The race covers a total distance of about 3500 km! Lance Armstrong from the USA holds the record of winning this event 7 times.

What did the first motorcycle look like?

In 1885 Gottlieb Daimler invented a motorcycle powered by a gas engine. It was a wooden bike fitted with an Otto cycle engine developed in 1876. These vehicles were popularly called 'bone shakers' owing to the jarring, bumpy rides they provided!

What was the first self-propelled vehicle ever invented?

In 1769, a French engineer and mechanic, Nicholas Joseph Cugnot invented a tractor capable of propelling itself. It was powered by steam engine and had to stop every ten to fifteen minutes to build up steam pressure. The vehicle ran on three wheels and was built for the French army to carry artillery.

When were electric cars invented?

In Scotland, between 1832 and 1839, the first electric carriage was invented by Robert Anderson. These cars were fitted with batteries to power the electric motor and the batteries needed to be recharged frequently. They were heavy, slow and expensive.

What did Charles Goodyear invent?

In 1844, Charles Goodyear invented vulcanized rubber that created a revolution in the manufacture of tyres. The process of vulcanization made car tyres waterproof, smooth and at the same time tough. Automobile tyres were made using this material because they provided a smooth ride and did not wear out easily.

Which was the first-known school bus?

It is believed that the first school bus was introduced in 1827 to shuttle children from home to school. It was a horse-drawn carriage introduced by George Shillibeer for a Quaker School in London.

How does the taxi get its name?

Cabs have a device called a taximeter which is used for calculating the fare that a customer should be charged, based on the distance travelled and speed of the vehicle. It was this device that gave the taxi cab its name!

Which is the longest train journey?

The Trans Siberian Express that runs between Moscow and Vladivostok in Russia is considered to be the longest train journey. The total length of the journey is about 9297 km!

What are some special features of Viking ships?

The Vikings built strong ships that were very advanced for their time and were considered to be one of the greatest technical advancements during the dark ages in Europe. These longships were lighter and more efficient than ships that existed at that time. These ships usually had dragon or serpent head on the prow because the superstitious Vikings believed that it would frighten away sea monsters and spirits!

What is significant about the ship, Mayflower?

The ship, Mayflower, has historic significance because it carried the pilgrims from England to Massachusetts in America in 1620. Originally built for carrying cargo and not passengers, the Mayflower carried 102 passengers during its historic journey! A replica of the original Mayflower was built in England in 1957 and given to America as a token of goodwill.

What was the ship on which Charles Darwin made his historic journey?

The HMS Beagle was a research ship on which Charles Darwin made his legendary journey to many places including the famous Galápagos Islands where he found many exotic plants and creatures. The journey began in 1831 and the entire voyage took 5 years.

What are bulk carriers?

Bulk carriers are cargo ships that are used to transport bulk cargo items such as ore or food. You can recognize it by the large box-like hatches on its deck, designed to slide outboard for loading.

What are tankers?

Tankers are cargo ships that are used for the transport of fluids, such as crude oil, petroleum products, liquefied petroleum gas, liquefied natural gas and chemicals, vegetable oils, wine and other foodstuffs.

What are container ships?

Container ships are cargo ships. They carry the entire load in truck-size containers in a technique called containerization. Informally known as "box boats," they carry the majority of the world's dry cargo. Most container ships are propelled by diesel engines, and have crews of between only 10 to 30 people.

What are Roll-On / Roll-Off ships?

Roll-on/Roll-off ships are cargo ships that are designed to carry cargo such as automobiles, trailers or railway carriages. RORO vessels have built-in ramps which allow the cargo to be efficiently "rolled on" and "rolled off" the vessel when in port, hence the name!

What are ferries?

Ferries are usually boats or ships used as a form of transport - it can carry people, and sometimes even their vehicles from one place to the other. Since most ferries travel rather short distances, they operate on regular, frequent return services and in places like Venice they are sometimes called water buses or water taxis.

What are reefers?

Reefer ships are also cargo ships, but ones that are specifically used for transportation of perishable commodities which require temperature-controlled transportation - mostly fruits, meat, fish, vegetables, dairy products and other perishable foodstuffs.

What are cruise ships?

Cruise ships are passenger ships that are used for pleasure voyages where the voyage itself and the ship's amenities are considered an essential part of the experience. Cruising has become a major part of the tourism industry with thousands of people cruising every year.

BY AIR

What is air travel?

Air travel is a form of travel that includes airplanes, helicopters, hot air balloons, blimps, gliders, parachutes or anything else that can prolong being in the air for sometime without crashing or being pulled by the earth's gravity. Since the Wright brothers' first flight in 1903, people have created a multitude of aircraft types.

How does an airplane take off?

When an aircraft moves, some air travels above the wing of the aircraft, and some below the wing. The shape of the wing creates lower air pressure above the wing. The higher air pressure under the wing lifts the plane into the air. When there is enough lift to overcome the plane's weight, the plane takes off. As long as the plane continues to move forward at a rapid speed, the plane continues to stay aloft!

When did people start flying in hot air balloons?

The hot air balloon is the oldest successful flight technology that could lift people. On Nov 21, 1783, in Paris, France, the first manned flight was made by Jean-François Pilâtre de Rozier and François Laurent d'Arlandes in a hot air balloon created on Dec 14, 1782 by the Montgolfier brothers.

What are civil aircraft?

All airplanes that carry cargo and passengers on board are known as civil aircraft. These include private jets, business planes and commercial airliners.

What is a military aircraft?

A military aircraft is any aircraft that is operated by an armed service of any type. A military aircraft can either be a combat or non-combat aircraft.

What are combat aircraft?

Combat aircraft are designed especially to destroy enemy equipment using armament that they have on board. Combat aircraft are normally developed and procured only by and for military forces.

What are fighters?

Fighters are used for destroying enemy aircraft in air-to-air combat, offensive or defensive. Many are fast and highly maneuverable. They are also used for escorting bombers or other aircraft and are also capable of carrying a variety of weapons including machine guns, cannons, rockets and guided missiles.

What are bombers?

Bombers are normally larger and heavier, and are capable of carrying large number of bombs. Generally bombers are used for ground attacks and are not as fast or agile enough to take on enemy fighters head-to-head. A few require one pilot to operate and others are larger and require a crew of two or more.

What are attack aircraft?

Attack aircraft are used to provide support for friendly ground troops. Some are able to carry regular or nuclear weapons far behind enemy lines to strike priority ground targets. Attack helicopters attack enemy armour and provide close air support for ground troops.

What are non-combat aircraft?

Non-combat aircraft are military aircraft which are used for search and rescue, reconnaissance, observation, surveillance, transport, training and aerial refueling. Although these aircraft are not designed for combat in their primary state, they can however carry weapons for self-defense. These mainly operate in support roles, and may be developed by either military forces or civilian organizations.

TRAVEL INTO SPACE

When did humans first attempt to travel into space?

The space age, the period when spacecraft were placed in the orbit around the Earth, began on October 4, 1957 when the Soviet Union launched Sputnik I, the first artificial satellite (an object that orbits a planet). At that time, the Soviet premier, Nikita Krushchev (1894–1971) immediately approved funds for follow-up space projects.

Who was the first person to travel into space?

On the 12th of April 1961, Russian cosmonaut Yuri Gagarin became the first human in space. He made a 108 minute orbital flight in his Vostok 1 spacecraft. Almost all the newspapers across the world trumpeted Gagarin's accomplishment!

Who was the first man on the moon?

On July 20, 1969, Neil Armstrong became the first human to step on the moon. He and Buzz Aldrin walked on the surface of the moon for around three hours. They performed experiments and picked up bits of moon dirt and rocks. They also put the American flag on the surface of the moon. Since then other astronauts have walked upon the moon surface!

What is a rocket?

The rocket was invented in China in the 1200's for fireworks! It is a tall, thin, cylindrical vehicle. It also refers to a missile, spacecraft, aircraft or other vehicle thrust upwards from a rocket engine. In all rockets, the exhaust is formed entirely from propellants carried within the rocket.

What is the Phoenix Lander?

The Phoenix Lander landed in the polar region of Mars on May 25, 2008 and it operated until November 10, 2008. Its mission was to search for a 'habitable zone' and to study the geological history of water on Mars. The Lander has a 2.5 metre robotic arm capable of digging shallow trenches.

What was the Space Shuttle?

The Space Shuttle was a reusable launch pad and an orbital spacecraft operated by the U.S. National Aeronautics and Space Administration (NASA) for human spaceflight missions. It included a rocket launcher, orbital spacecraft and re-entry space plane with modular add-ons. The first test flights and operational flights began in 1982, all launched from the Kennedy Space Center in Florida.

What is the International Space Station?

The International Space Station (ISS) is an internationally-developed research facility that was assembled in the lower part of the Earth's orbit. It is the largest space station ever constructed. In-orbit construction of the station began in 1998 and is scheduled to be completed by 2012. Like many artificial satellites, the ISS can be seen from Earth with the naked eye. The ISS serves as a research laboratory where crews conduct experiments in biology, chemistry, physics, astronomy and meteorology.

Who was the first space tourist?

Dennis Tito, an American millionaire, became the first space tourist. He paid 20 million dollars in 2001 to get a ride in a Russian Soyuz spacecraft. He spent a week in orbit and visited the International Space Station!

Which spacecraft has traveled beyond the solar system?

Voyager 1 and 2 were launched in 1977 to explore the regions beyond our Solar System. These spacecraft have travelled a distance much farther than Pluto. Although they were initially launched to explore Jupiter and Saturn, the mission was extended to explore the outer planets, Uranus and Neptune and the farther realms of the Solar System!

What are satellites used for?

Satellites are man-made objects that orbit around the earth and are used for many purposes like research, communication, weather forecast and navigation assistance. These satellites have solar-power cells that convert solar energy into electricity.

FILMS

What was there to entertain people before films?

A thousand years before films existed, plays and dances were organized to entertain people. They had many elements common to films - scripts, sets, lighting, costumes, production, direction, actors, audiences, storyboards and scores.

What is a film?

A film, a movie or motion picture is a series of still or moving images. Films are made up of a series of individual images called frames. When these images are shown rapidly in succession, a viewer has the illusion that motion is occurring. The viewer cannot see the flickering between frames because of an effect called the persistence of vision, where the eye retains a visual image for a fraction of a second after the source has been removed.

What was a silent film?

For the first thirty years of their history, films were silent because inventors and producers could not make films where the image could match the sound, although in most cases it was accompanied by live musicians and sometimes sound effects and even some commentary by the showman or projectionist.

Which was the first film in colour?

It is believed that the first full length commercial colour film was 'The World, the Flesh and the Devil' made in Britain in 1914 It was produced by the Union Jack Company.

Which was the first ever 3D movie?

Power of Love released in 1922 is considered to be the first 3D movie. However, The House of Wax, a horror movie released in 1953, is considered to be the first ever major 3D studio feature to gain popularity. Did you know that in the early 3D movies, people actually found that the wobbly images caused headaches and made them feel ill!

What is commercial cinema?

Mainstream or commercial cinema is produced with the intention to make money and with a commercial interest associated with it and generally has mass appeal.

What is art cinema?

Art or Parallel Cinema is an alternative to commercial cinema. It is a specific movement where subjects are more serious and art-related and also had a keen and critical eye on the social and political situation of the times.

What is a blockbuster movie?

The term blockbuster has been used to describe a commercial movie's hit at the box office. In the 1970's words used to describe it were spectacular, super-grosser and super-blockbuster. In 1975 the usage of 'blockbuster' for films was synonymous with Steven Spielberg's Jaws. It was seen as something new: a cultural phenomenon with fast-paced exciting entertainment. Audiences often raved about them afterwards, and went back to see them again just for the thrill!

What is a mini-series?

A mini-series is a television show production which tells a story in a planned limited number of episodes. The exact number would depend on limited episodes that made a season. The term 'miniseries' is generally a North American term with the British equivalent of 'serials'.

What are some famous awards given to exceptional actors?

These are some prestigious awards for outstanding actors and actresses across the world:

- Oscar Award
- Golden Globe Award
- Bafta Award
- Cannes Film Festival Award

COMPUTERS AND THE INTERNET

Which was the first computer game?

Alexander Douglas is credited with creating the first ever graphic computer game, back in 1952! The game was a version of Tic Tac Toe and it was programmed on a vacuum tube computer with a cathode ray tube display.

What is a laptop?

A laptop is a personal computer for mobile use. In a laptop, you have the same components of a desktop computer, which includes a processor, display, a keyboard, a pointing device or a touchpad and speakers all in a single unit. A laptop is powered by an AC adapter that charges an internal rechargeable battery. Generally, a laptop battery can store energy to run the laptop for three to five hours.

What is a net book?

A net book is a laptop that is light-weight, economical, energy-efficient and one which is especially suited for wireless communication and Internet access. With a primary focus given to web browsing and emailing, a net book relies heavily on the Internet for remote access to web-based applications.

When was the internet invented?

The original idea of networking through computers was envisioned by JCR Licklider, way back in 1962. More than 40 years ago, the US Defence department set up the ARPANET (a precursor for the internet) to link up different networks, mainly for government and scientific use. By 1992 internet access was available to the common public and it has become indispensable today!

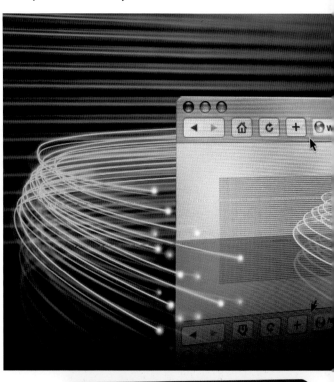

What are search engines?

Search engines are designed to help us search specific information from the large pool of resources available in the World Wide Web. You type in specific keywords and the search engine displays all results that match the keyword, all in a matter of a few seconds! Some well-known search engines include Google, Alta Vista, Yahoo Search, Bing and Dogpile!

What was the first ever email sent?

It is said that Ray Tomlinson, an engineer, was the first person to send an email in 1971! Before this, people could send messages only to users on a single machine. Tomlinson achieved a breakthrough by sending messages to other machines on the internet using the symbol '@' to designate the receiving machine!

What is a computer virus?

A computer virus is a computer program written intentionally and that can attach itself to any other programs. The 'virus' is hidden in the programs that are most widely and commonly used so that it can spread very quickly. A virus does not cause any harm to your computer until the infected program is executed or if a disk containing infected files is used.

How do anti-virus programs work?

Most anti-virus software have inbuilt virus dictionaries – they examine programs and documents in the computer and look for known viruses from the dictionary. In another approach, it looks for any suspicious program activity– for instance, to find if there are any programs trying to write data or to send data. The anti-virus then alerts the user about its find and the suspicious program or file can be deleted or repaired.

What is a website?

A website is a collection of web pages that contain images, videos or other digital assets. A website is hosted on at least one web server and can be accessible through a network such as the Internet. All websites that are publicly accessible constitute the World Wide Web.

What is a social networking service?

A social networking service is an online service or website which helps in building social networks or social relations among people, who share interests or activities. A social network service consists of a representation of each user, called a profile, social links and a variety of additional services. One of these sites that have taken the world by storm is Facebook. Other popular networking sites are: Google +, Twitter, Orkut and MySpace.

THE WARS

What is war?

War is an armed conflict between two opposing states, nationalities or other groups (e.g. guerillas). It can occur for a prolonged period of time and result in destruction of lives and property on a large scale.

What is guerilla warfare?

It refers to a type of conflict in which the war is fought by guerillas. Guerillas are irregular combatants who do not belong to the government or the military forces. They wage small-scale warfare against existing government, military or police forces and occasionally with rival groups.

What is Conventional warfare?

In simple terms, conventional warfare is an open battle involving direct attacks by armed forces. It happens between two opposing states where the respective troops use military strategy and weapons to attack.

What is nuclear warfare?

A war that is waged where nuclear weapons are the main weapons used instead of weapons like guns, tanks and troops, to force or pressurize surrender of the opposing side is called nuclear warfare. The term nuclear warfare applies when nuclear weapons are used by both or all sides involved in the war.

What is a civil war?

A civil war refers to war between regions of the same country, people or political entity. These regions compete for control or independence from that nation. The most famous example is the American civil war where the twenty five states that formed the 'Union' fought against the southern states that formed the 'Confederacy' and defeated them which resulted in presidential election of 1860.

What was World War 1?

World War I, also called the First World War or Great War, was a major war in Europe that began in 1914 and lasted until 1918. The countries assembled in two opposing alliances: the Allies and the Central Powers. The central powers were Germany, Austria-Hungary, Bulgaria and Turkey. The allies were Britain, France, USA, Russia, Belgium, Serbia, Greece, Romania, Portugal, Italy, Japan and Montenegro. More than 70 million military personnel, including 60 million Europeans, were assembled in one of the largest wars in history where more than 9 million participants of the war were killed, largely because of great technological advances in firepower.

Barbed wire cut, Americans

When and why did World War II occur?

World War II began in September, 1939 and raged on until 1945. It began when Germany launched an unprovoked attack on Poland. Britain and France declared war on Germany but many countries were involved in the war. The allies consisted of 17 countries - Poland, Britain, France, USA, USSR, Australia, Belgium, Brazil, Canada, Denmark, Greece, China, Netherlands, Norway, South Africa, New Zealand and Yugoslavia. The axis powers were Germany, Japan, Italy, Hungary, Romania and Bulgaria. Considered one of the deadliest war, more than 100 million people fought in it and it is estimated that about 50 – 70 million people lost their lives!

Who are paratroopers?

Paratroopers are specially-trained soldiers who attack after parachuting down from airplanes. Also called airborne troops, paratroopers train to jump from airplanes, open their chutes, land on ground and instantly start to fight. Germany and Russia developed the first paratroopers during World War I.

What do you mean by the term government?

The term government refers to the legislators and administrators who represent the people and help to carry out the administration and control a state at a given time. A stable government is necessary for the existence of a civilized and orderly society.

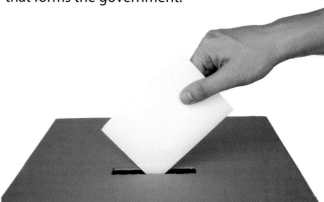

What is constitutional monarchy?

Constitutional monarchy is a 'limited monarchy' - a form of government where the monarch acts as the head of state according to the constitution of the country. But the monarch does not wield absolute power and is only responsible for ceremonial duties or may have certain powers, depending on the constitution, while the prime minister chosen by the people wields the actual power. The UK is an example of a constitutional monarchy.

What does constitutional republic mean?

A constitutional republic is a form of government where the head of state and other officials are elected by the people and are true representatives of the people. They must govern according to the existing constitutional law, which ensures that the representatives cannot misuse their powers. An example of this kind of government is the American government.

What is a democracy?

A democracy is another word to describe a government that is ruled by the people and for the people. It is generally a constitutional republic or a constitutional monarchy where a political party that secures the largest number of votes is the one that forms the government.

What does the term 'authoritarian government' mean?

An Authoritarian Government is a system of government that is controlled by a group of people who are not really elected by the people. Under this government, the process of voting is often tampered. The government is controlled by people who care little about civil liberties and only support groups that will propagate their own political agenda.

What is a Dictator?

A dictator is a Latin word which means 'one who commands'. Indeed, a dictator takes command of an entire nation and the dictator wields power over the country, which is usually acquired purely by force. It can also happen when a dictator acquires power by the accepted rules of the constitution but amends the constitution to control the country on their own and gather all power to themselves. An example of this kind of government was that led by Idi Amin in Uganda.

What is oligarchy?

It is a form of government in which all the power is vested in a select group of people distinguished by royalty, wealth, physical traits or some other special privileges. This group decides the rules and laws that should govern that country. Oligarchy occurred in South Africa during Apartheid.

What is Anarchy?

Anarchy is a condition where there isn't any kind of government. This can happen after a civil war in a country. The existing government is rendered powerless and there are rival groups fighting to take control over the country.

What is Theocracy?

Theocracy is a form of government where the state or nation is governed by divine guidance and especially a state ruled by officials who are regarded as 'divinely guided'. In such sates it is 'God himself who is recognized as the head of the state'. An example of this kind of government is found in the Vatican City where the Pope exercises power.

GLOBAL WARMING

What is global warming?

Global warming is the gradual rising of Earth's temperature - a rise that is greater than anything humans have faced in recent history. Unless this is tackled soon, this rise could transform the planet we live on. This temperature rise could make our planet's climate change so much that it could force many species to extinction!

How much has the temperature risen?

A number of things that people do year after year make the planet warmer. Although Earth has only warmed up by around 0.8 °C in the 1900's, it is predicted that by the end of the 21st century, global warming is likely to cause an increase in Earth's temperature of around 2–5 °C. Once something as big as a planet starts to warm up, it is very hard to slow down the process and almost impossible to stop it completely!

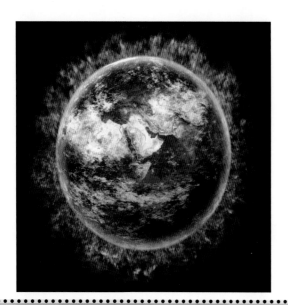

What is natural greenhouse effect?

The atmosphere has a number of gases that trap the heat given out by the Earth to make sure that the Earth's temperature remains constant. This process is called the natural greenhouse effect. Without it, the Earth would be much too cold to support the huge diversity of life that it does.

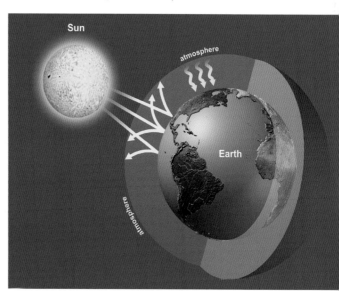

What are the greenhouse gases?

Greenhouse gases are found in the atmosphere and trap the heat radiated from Earth. Carbon dioxide, methane, nitrous oxide, ozone and water vapour are the major greenhouse gases.

What is enhanced greenhouse effect?

Some of the activities of humans also produce greenhouse gases. With time, these gases keep building up in the atmosphere thus disrupting the balance of the greenhouse gases. This can have a drastic effect on the whole planet. Burning fossil fuels like coal, oil and natural gas releases carbon dioxide into the atmosphere. Cutting down and burning trees also produces a lot of carbon dioxide. As more and more greenhouse gases get released into the atmosphere, more heat is trapped thus making the Earth warmer. A lot of scientists agree that if we continue polluting the atmosphere with greenhouse gases, it will have very dangerous effect on the Earth.

How does global warming affect the oceans?

Global warming causes the sea level to rise and as a result the water covers many islands destroying living things dependent on the island. The rising temperatures kill algae in the oceans. The algae are the primary food for many living things in the ocean. This in turn threatens the survival of sea creatures that depend on algae and eventually the entire marine food cycle.

How is the polar region affected by global warming?

An increase in temperature causes the polar ice caps and glaciers to melt. Creatures adapted to living in the polar regions, like penguins and polar bears, have difficulty adjusting to the rise in temperature. It also increasingly becomes difficult for them to find food. As a result, the population of polar animals and birds is slowly diminishing.

Is global warming getting worse?

As a result of the fossil fuels we burn there is now more carbon dioxide in the atmosphere than at any time in the last 420,000 years! With more heat trapped on Earth, the planet will become warmer, leading to a change in weather all over the Earth with summers getting hotter and winters warmer. This large rise in temperature could harm us and other living things on Earth.

What can we do to stop global warming?

The answer lies in reducing the impact of climate change by reducing global warming. This would mean reducing carbon dioxide emissions and using energy more efficiently. Some things that people can do are to replace normal light bulbs with energy-saving fluorescent lamps. One can cycle, walk, or take the bus instead of using cars. People can use natural means of cooling the house instead of using air conditioners and use renewable energy.

NUCLEAR POWER

What is Nuclear energy?

Nuclear energy is the energy in the nucleus or the core of an atom. The nucleus of an atom contains positively charged protons and neutral neutrons. Electrons with a negative charge revolve around this nucleus. A lot of energy is stored in the bonds that hold atoms together. Nuclear fission and nuclear fusion are the two processes which release the energy stored in the nucleus. Nuclear energy or nuclear power is a clean and safe way to make electricity. Unlike coal, it does not burn, so there are no pollutants or gases released into the air.

What is Nuclear Fusion?

Nuclear fusion is a way of combining the atoms to make a new atom. Inside the sun, hydrogen atoms combine together to produce helium. Because helium does not need that much energy to hold it together, the extra energy that is produced is released as heat and light.

How do nuclear plants generate electricity?

Nuclear power plants use fission to make electricity. By splitting uranium atoms into two smaller atoms, the extra energy is released as heat. Since uranium is considerably cheap and plentiful, it is used by power plants to make electricity. Fission creates heat that boils water into steam inside a reactor. The steam then turns huge turbines that drive generators to make electricity. The steam is then converted back into water and cooled down in a cooling tower. The water can then be used over and over again.

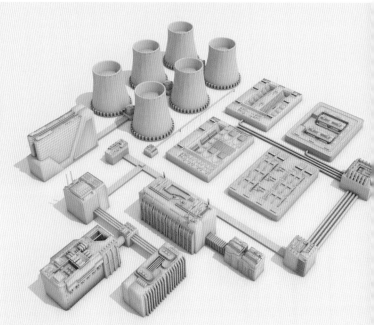

What is Fission?

Nuclear Fission is a way of splitting an atom into two smaller atoms. Because of their size, the smaller atoms don't need as much energy to hold them together as the larger atom, so the extra energy is released as heat and radiation.

How is nuclear radiation used?

Nuclear radiation can either be extremely beneficial or extremely dangerous - it just depends on how it is used. In cases where it is beneficial, it is used in X-ray machines for diagnosis and nuclear power plants for generating energy whereas it is also used in nuclear weapons - a dangerous source of destruction.

What are the advantages and disadvantages of nuclear energy?

Nuclear energy is produced in large quantities using small amounts of fuel. It does not produce a lot of waste and does not release pollutants into the atmosphere. On the other hand, nuclear plants have to be protected as any leak of radioactive substance can be extremely harmful to humans and other living things. Whatever waste is generated, needs to be buried and sealed for hundreds of years until it loses its radioactivity.

Can nuclear radiation be dangerous?

Yes! Too much of nuclear radiation can lead to cell damage. It can damage the DNA inside the cells through its ionizing effect. A common example is sunburn that is caused by ultraviolet light. Over-radiation can lead to melanoma and other forms of cancer. Exposure to very high doses of radiation can even kill living beings.

What is radioactive waste?

The residue of nuclear power and energy is called radioactive waste. It is of high concern to the environment because even ordinary trash comprising of tools, protective clothing, wiping cloths and disposables, have been contaminated with small amounts of radioactive dust or particles. So, they have to be stored in specially designed dry storage containers so as not to come in contact with the outside environment.

Which is considered to be the worst nuclear disaster in the world?

The Chernobyl nuclear accident that happened in April, 1986 is regarded as the worst nuclear accident in history. It was the first nuclear accident to be classified as a 'major accident' by the International Atomic Energy Agency. Several people died due to radiation exposure and people who lived in the vicinity were relocated to other areas due to the high levels of radioactive contamination surrounding the reactor site.

ENDANGERED HABITATS AND SPECIES

What is a habitat?

A habitat is where an animal, bird or insect lives. It not only means its home but the entire area that it uses. For an animal, a habitat includes all the land the animal needs to hunt, gather food, find a mate and raise a family. The habitat provides the animal with food, water, space and shelter.

What is habitat destruction?

Habitat destruction is the process where the natural habitat of a certain animal, bird or insect is functionally unable to support the species any more. The species which previously used the site is forced to leave or is destroyed, thus reducing their number. Main causes of habitat destruction are cutting trees, setting up industries, farming and urbanization.

What are endangered species?

An endangered species is a population of organisms or species that is at risk of becoming extinct because its existence has been threatened by changing environmental conditions. As a result, their number has drastically reduced compared to the numbers that existed before. Presently there are more than 1,000 animal species that are endangered worldwide, and this figure is ever increasing.

When did species begin to disappear?

Ever since life began there have always been species that have been endangered. These species slowly disappeared because of changes in the climate and that particular species' inability to adapt to such conditions. Although extinction is a natural part of evolution, the number of species dying out every year has risen drastically since the 15th century. Humans have been an important factor in causing many bird and animal species to go extinct. It is predicted that 50,000 species will become extinct by the turn of the century.

How does hunting for food and fur affect the habitat today?

Since the 15th century, the commercial exploitation of animals for food and other natural products is the root cause for many species becoming endangered or extinct. Look at the slaughtering of the great whales for oil and meat and how the African rhinos were killed for their horns. Scientists believe that the dodos were also hunted to extinction!

How does pollution contribute to endangering our habitat?

Pollution is a major risk to many species. Toxic chemicals like dichloro-diphenyl-trichloroethane (DDT) and polychlorinated biphenyls (PCB's) used as pesticides interfere with the calcium metabolism of birds, causing soft-shelled eggs and malformed young. PCB's also impair reproduction in some animals. Water pollution and increased water temperatures have killed fish in several habitats.

What are conservationists?

Conservationists help preserve the Earth's diversity by applying scientific knowledge and technology to solve environment problems. This includes protecting animal species, their habitats and by encouraging the use of renewable resources.

What have organizations and governments done to help save declining species?

Across the world, private and governmental efforts have been adopted to save declining species. One really effective and immediate approach to protect a species, is by legislation. Countries all over the world make laws to ensure that there are mechanisms for the conservation of ecosystems upon which endangered species depend. The International Trade in Endangered Species of Wild Fauna and Flora, ratified by 51 nations, restricts exploitation of wildlife and plants by regulating and restricting trade in species.

What is Greenpeace?

Greenpeace is a privately run and funded worldwide organization that was formed to bring environmental problems like animal poaching, dangers of nuclear reactors and genetic engineering to the attention of the world. Greenpeace has been actively campaigning against the killing of whales and other animals. This organization attempts to act as a conscience for the world. It monitors how governments and multinational corporations behave towards the environment.

GO GREEN

What does the term 'Go Green' mean?

Although we have heard the phrase "Go Green" many times before, most people don't understand the real concept of it. People mistake going green with being a "tree hugger". The actual meaning of going green is much more about caring for the environment and to take an active part in doing so. An example of going green would be carrying a few canvas sacks when one goes to the grocery store instead of carrying plastic bags, which are dangerous to the environment and cannot be easily recycled.

What are the three R's of conservation?

The "3R's" is a famous term that is used especially to describe the three ways by which you can help produce less waste. It is often symbolized by three arrows, arranged in a triangle. The 3R's are: Reduce, Reuse and Recycle.

What is Reduce?

The word reduce in the 3R's of conservation simply means throwing away less. This would mean purchasing long-lasting goods that come in smaller packaging. Buy only what you need and make maximum use of it before throwing it away. A good example is to buy stuff in bulk instead of individual packets – this means less plastic or paper wrapping material is thrown away!

What does Reuse mean?

Another way of managing waste is by reusing old items. Think twice before you throw something away. This includes repairing items, donating them to charity groups or using them in a different way. For example, most electrical products can be repaired by replacing the necessary parts, while things like old clothes or toys can be donated to people who are less fortunate and old bottles can be used as home-made plant pots.

What does Recycle mean?

Recycling is the most important process when it comes to a waste reduction strategy. It is a method where materials that would otherwise become waste are converted into valuable items. By recycling, we can play a part in conserving the Earth and its resources. The recycling process involves the collection of recyclable materials, sorting and processing them and manufacturing them into new products.

How are goods recycled?

Recyclable materials are collected from homes, schools, colleges and work places. They are then taken to recycling centers where they are sorted into their material type. These raw materials are sometimes called 'recyclables'. They are then sold to manufacturing companies where these recyclables are made into a variety of products.

What are some products made from recycled goods?

Today you can get many products that are totally or partially made of recycled content. Examples are newspapers, plastic bottles and metal soft drink cans.

What do you do by purchasing recycled products?

You do a great favour to the environment and make the recycling process a success by purchasing recycled goods! When more people like you start demanding environmentally friendly goods, the manufacturers have to meet the demand by producing more of it! This would encourage the process of recycling and lead to a cleaner environment!

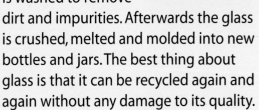

How is glass recycled?

Glass from the recycle bin is taken to a glass treatment plant where it is sorted by colour first. Then the glass is washed to remove dirt and impurities. Afterwards the glass is crushed, melted and molded into new bottles and jars. The best thing about glass is that it can be recycled again and again without any damage to its quality.